The
Pink
Dress

The Pink Dress

BY ANNE ALEXANDER

GRAYMALKIN
MEDIA

Dedicated to my daughter,

Sharon

with love.

Published by Graymalkin Media

www.graymalkin.com

Originally published by Doubleday & Company, Inc.

This edition published in 2016 by Graymalkin Media

ISBN: 978-1-63168-036-6

Printed in the United States of America

5 7 9 10 8 6 4

Designed by Timonthy Shaner

Contents

Foreword

I was in the eighth grade in 1956 and my mother, Anne Alexander, was writing a book. My friends and I loved it. It was about US. The challenges Sue Stevens struggled with in the story were issues we faced in real life.

A few of my girlfriends walked home from school with me every day, anxious to find out what would happen next in *The Pink Dress*. My mother promised she would have a new chapter ready, and she never let us down. We girls sat in a circle and passed typed pages around. We read fervently, smiled sometimes, wiped tears from our cheeks, and rooted for our heroine. We were the first of many readers to meet and care about Sue and Dave, Judy and Mo, and the other characters in the book.

If this is your first time reading *The Pink Dress*, welcome! The original middle-school readers and I are grandmothers now, and some of us are still friends. We are pleased that our daughters and granddaughters love *The Pink Dress* as much as we did. I bet you'll love it too.

—SHARON ALEXANDER WILLIAMS

The Pink Dress

1

Peppermint Prom

IT STARTED WITH THE pink dress. The dress hung from the wall bracket in her room, with all its starched, pretty newness waiting and ready for her to slip it on. Sue couldn't keep from looking at it and touching it as she got ready for the dance.

It seemed almost unbelievable that she, Susan Stevens, was going to a school dance at last. As Mom sewed the dress during the week, Sue had wondered just what would happen this time to make her miss the party. She'd lost out on the Halloween dance because of a leg injury. She'd been kept from the Christmas dance by the flu. But tonight . . . she twirled with the joy of it all, and her many petticoats swished out in a scalloped circle.

Peppermint Prom sounded like such a *fun* name for a dance. It sounded so sort of *swish*. And—she eyed her dress again—her dress was just the delectable shade of a pink

1

peppermint wafer. Prickles of excitement made Sue feel like dancing around the room in leaps and twirls as she used to when she took ballet. Instead, she settled herself before her dressing table, took out the bobby pins, and started to brush her hair. As she counted the strokes, she heard feet on the stairs, and Jay and Kit burst into her room.

"Mommie says that Daddy says it's almost time," four-year-old Kit announced.

"Okay." Sue looked at her little sister. Kit had such a long way to go before she would be a ninth grader and a teen-ager and getting ready for a dance. Poor little kid.

Jay plunked himself on the bed with the complete unconcern of a six-year-old boy. He jabbed at the hunk of modeling clay he held in his hand while Sue dabbed perfume behind her ears and along the part in her hair. She dabbed some on Kit, too, and offered the bottle to Jay to smell. He sniffed. "Girls do silly stuff," he commented.

Boys were the silly ones, Sue wanted to amend. But this was no time to get into an argument with Jay. She slipped her dress off the hanger and popped it over her head, wiggling her way into it. What would Jay be like when he got older, she wondered. Maybe he'd be like Dave—Dave Young, who transferred to Taft last September. The way Dave had slipped into leadership of The Crowd, one would think he'd known the others for years. Jay better not get into the *difficulties* Dave did, though. Dave was in the opposite wing of classrooms from her, so Sue didn't know him to speak to, and about the only time she ever saw him was when he was going in or out of the principal's office. *That,* anyone would admit, was quite often.

"Move, Kit," Sue demanded. Boys might be silly, but little girls were pests. They always managed to be exactly where one wanted to step.

Kit allowed her an inch more space by the mirror. Sue applied her lipstick—*Pink Paradise*—in careful strokes. Some girls in ninth grade already had lipstick brushes. Sue felt she was lucky to be allowed to wear any at all.

"Need any help?" Mom called from downstairs.

"All ready." Sue scooped up her white cardigan from the chair and draped it over her shoulders.

As she stood before her parents in the living room for a last-minute inspection, Mom snipped at a stray thread. "Stand tall," she said. "Stand proud."

Sue managed a rueful grin. Stand tall? She was tall—just about the tallest girl in Taft Junior High. Most of the boys seemed to stand short. She straightened her shoulders and gave an experimental twirl. "Do I look okay?"

Dad gave a wolf growl of approval. Mom said. "I think you look lovely." Jay reserved comment, but Kit put her face up for a kiss. "I think you look like a princess," she said.

Sue laughed. Leave it to Kit for the extravagant praise. If only she *could* look like a princess. But everything about her was so *ordinary*—from her betwixt and between brown hair to her blue eyes. She even had a "healthy" (as Dad termed it) sprinkling of freckles.

Now Dad shrugged into his coat and walked with her to the car. Sue waved her good-bys as they backed out the driveway. The prickles of excitement gave way to clammy chills of apprehension. What if she didn't get asked for a single dance?

"We'll pick up Cathy first," Dad said. He rounded the corner, and Sue was glad that at least she didn't have to walk into the dance alone. Cathy and Ellen would be with her.

When Dad stopped in front of her classmate's house, Cathy was already running down the steps. She giggled as Dad opened the door for her.

"Good evening, Cathy," he said. "My, don't we look pretty tonight."

"Hi, Mr. Stevens." Cathy giggled again as she hopped into the car. "Isn't this exciting?" she asked Sue.

"I'm scared," Sue admitted. "What if I don't get *asked?*"

"Oh, pooh." Cathy dismissed the thought. "Someone will ask you."

Yes, someone would. There was tubby, waddly John who tried to ask every girl at every dance. He'd ask her for sure. And then there was Chester. He'd ask because they went to dancing school together. If only he weren't so short. And of course there was Ricky. He was the best of her three possibilities. If only he enjoyed dancing instead of seeming mortally wounded every time he asked you. Ricky wanted to be a doctor someday, and he just couldn't see what dancing had to do with doctoring. If his mother didn't insist, Sue knew he'd never be at any social function.

"Hi." Ellen's greeting jerked Sue from her thoughts. Goodness, she hadn't even realized Dad had stopped at Ellen's. She barely had time to give an answering. "Hi," it seemed, before they were at the school, at dear old Taft.

"Leave some dancing partners for the other girls," Dad joked. "And, Sue," he added, "don't forget to say hello to the chaperons."

"I won't," she promised.

"Glad our parents didn't think of that," said Cathy when they were out of earshot.

Sue wished fervently Dad hadn't thought of it, too. Good manners, Dad always insisted, never hurt anybody. But sometimes she couldn't see it. Good manners often meant standing at the end of a line, or getting the piece of cake with the least icing.

She trailed up the steps to the gymnasium behind Cathy and Ellen. Oh, if only her heart would stop pounding. She stopped at the door and gaped. This the gym? Why, it was hardly recognizable—it was like a fairyland with the peppermint candy decorations and the pink and white streamers. Up there at the ceiling were hundreds of balloons. And the music—an orchestra—real live music! Wasn't this wonderful?

"Come on." Cathy tugged at her. "You're blocking the door."

As the three moved through the doorway, they became a part of the cluster of girls who clung to the wall like so many moths around a light. Sue noticed that on the other side of the hall the boys stood in a sort of disorganized huddle, a little bit like moths, too. And out there on the floor were the brave ones, the lucky ones, dancing. Well, no one could expect her to be dancing yet. She'd just got here.

Intermission descended upon the three girls as they exchanged niceties on their dresses. Cute, petite Cathy looked darling in her yellow striped, and Ellen—well, blue always had been her best color.

"I—I wish we could make them ask girls to dance"

"It's intermission, dopey." Sue scanned the crowd of boys, looking for a familiar face. "They'll ask." She could see Dave Young, and he was as good-looking as ever. But where was Ricky—or Chester?

"They didn't last time," said Cathy.

"Didn't what?" Sue turned to her friend.

"Ask."

"Oh no," Sue moaned. "Won't the chaperons do something?"

Ellen and Cathy shook their heads. Conversation rose around them like the swell of the ocean's roar. The voices made even the paper candy canes quiver, and Sue wondered why the high-pitched giggles didn't pierce the balloons and pop them.

Then the orchestra sounded above the babble, and it was amazing how quickly some of the girls were asked—like ducks in a shooting gallery. And then John waddled up to ask Cathy—and Chester came for Ellen. "Ricky will be over in a minute," Cathy said comfortingly. But Chester shook his head. "Huh-uh," he said. "Ricky couldn't come. His brother just got in from overseas."

For a moment Sue thought of going home. She made herself as small as she could against the wall, and was glad to note at least a few other girls were wallflowers like herself.

The next dance Chester asked her, and Sue, towering what seemed like *feet* instead of inches above him, did his methodical step-step-close in class-like precision. But that left Cathy standing against the wall alone. Because John had asked Ellen. At least, Sue told herself, I'll get two dances. There was still John.

Soon she was back at her post against the wall. Somehow the minutes that ticked by on the gym clock stretched out like rubber bands. Now it was the girls' choice—girls' tag. But even then she couldn't make herself move. She watched the crowd shifting rapidly. The girls weren't nearly so shy as the boys. The stag line over by the wall was rapidly being depleted. And there was Dave—*the* Dave—out in the middle of the floor, not getting more than two steps with each girl before another cut in.

Dave, the kids said, was going steady with Judy this week. Dave and Judy were the *good* kids in the school. Not good like good-behavior good, but the ones who ran things their way.

At the next intermission she took stock. Six dances—she'd had two. Just the one with Chester, the other with John. "Speak to the chaperons; have a lot of dances," Dad had said. Well, when the next dance started there'd be something to do—say hello to the chaperons.

The music started, and Sue edged along through the dancers toward the group of chaperons. She'd almost reached them when she suddenly collided with someone in the crowd.

"Sorry," Sue said automatically.

"Dance?" said a boy's voice. It was Dave. He was looking around with angry eyes.

"Dance?" Dave said again.

Sue looked in back of her.

"I mean *you!* In the pink dress." Dave held out his hand,

and Sue, her feet feeling like lumps of clay in her ballerinas, followed him onto the floor.

It took agonizing moments before she could follow Dave's steps. Desperately she wished he did Chester's staid step-step-close. But no, Dave was always putting in extras in the way of footwork.

She looked up at him—glad that for once she was dancing with a boy she could look up *at*. Dave's eyes seemed to be searching the crowd. Finally he seemed to catch someone's glance, because he smiled with almost a sneer, then he gave her his undivided attention. "Relax," he told her. "Relax."

When the piece ended, Sue sought frantically for a way to break without being awkward about it. Now she had something to remember—dancing with Dave. But she didn't want him to feel the least bit stuck with her.

"My friends are over there." She pointed to the sidelines and turned to join them. Boy-and-girl manners here didn't include the boy escorting you back, as he had to in dancing class.

"What's your hurry?" Dave drawled. "It's a jig now; let's go."

Jig? Oh no! She and Ellen and Cathy had tried it at home. And they thought they were pretty good at times. But they'd never, not ever, jigged with boys. Well, this would certainly teach Dave not to ask strange girls to dance. She laughed. "You don't even know my name," she told him. "I'm Sue—and I don't know whether I can jig."

"With me, you can do anything," said Dave. "And I know you're Sue—in wing nine-three."

Willing her feet to follow Dave's in the intricate steps, Sue found herself quite adept with the toe-heel, toe-heel, twist, swing. Swish-swish went the nice full skirt of the pink dress. And she found herself relaxing—if one could call it that in a jig.

"Cute dress," Dave commented on one of the whirls. "You don't jig bad for a beginner. I'll teach you a little."

Sue smothered a giggle. Dave was conceited, that was for sure. But he really could jig. The dance ended in a mad swirl of music and flying feet, and as the orchestra's last few notes spelled intermission, she looked up at the musicians. They looked exhausted too.

"My friends—they—they're over there," Sue told Dave again. She simply couldn't let him get stuck with her.

"We'll get a Coke," Dave said as though he hadn't heard her. She felt herself being pushed through the crowd to the soft-drinks booth. The kids parted like the Red Sea to let Dave through. Yes, he was just about the biggest thrill at Taft—and he was buying her a Coke!

As they stood there, sipping their Cokes with the crowd milling around, Sue saw Ellen and Cathy with John and

Chester in tow trying to make their way to the booth. "My friends," she said, as she took a couple of steps toward them. That, apparently, was all she had to do, for the girls came quickly toward her.

"Ellen, Cathy, Dave," she introduced them.

"Wings six-two and seven-four," Dave acknowledged.

And then, because John and Chester were there, too, Sue introduced them. Dave barely looked at the boys. The music started up again, and he took the bottle from her hand and tossed it to John. "Come on, let's go," he demanded.

Bossy character, this Dave. And rude, too. But Sue found herself matching her steps to his. And from then on she danced every dance with him. Except for girls' tag, of course, when Dave was tagged over and over again. Sue tagged Chester and then John. When she was back once again with Dave, he turned on her angrily. "Lay off those creeps," he demanded.

"What creeps?"

"Those jerks, John and Chester."

Sue started to protest when Dave was tagged in on again, and she found herself facing one of Dave's pals.

The boy didn't take Sue's proffered hand but merely glared at her. "Judy says lay off Dave," he warned her. "They're going steady."

Sue felt herself flush, but before she could think of a

suitable answer he'd turned away and was gone in the crowd. She tagged in on Dave determinedly.

"Are you?" she asked.

"Am I what?"

"Going steady with Judy."

"No." Dave's voice was angry. "But do you want to?"

Now it was Sue's turn to ask, "What?"

"Go steady—with me." The dance had ended now, and Dave stood facing her with a defiant look on his face.

Sue laughed. "I don't even *know* you."

"So?"

"So—no, of course."

"You will," Dave predicted confidently. He put his hand on her shoulder and guided her off the dance floor. "You will," he repeated.

Bossy, rude, AND *conceited,* Sue tabulated to herself. But that was nothing new. She'd known he had those characteristics before he even spoke to her. Why not just have fun and enjoy the dance now for what it offered?

The dance was almost over when Sue remembered about the chaperons. "I promised my dad," she said when Dave protested.

"He won't know—just say you did."

"But I promised." She broke away and went over to speak to them.

"Having fun?" Mrs. Smith asked.

"Dreamy," she told her. And it was true. She was having a dreamy time—even if Dave never spoke to her again after tonight. The dance was wonderful. And the minutes were whizzing by as swiftly as they'd dragged before.

"Mission accomplished?" Dave whirled her out on the dance floor again. Sue nodded. Mission accomplished? What was it Dad had said? Besides talking to the chaperons? *Leave some dancing partners for the other girls.* She was leaving them all—except for Dave. She could hardly believe it when the band swung into the good-night number.

The last chord sounded. Dave walked her over to Ellen and Cathy. "See you around," he said with a brief nod.

The three girls pushed their way to the steps to await their ride home.

"How did you rate?" Ellen asked. "Jeepers, he's cute."

"My dress," Sue answered. "He liked my pink dress."

"No." Cathy shook her head. "It wasn't the dress. He and Judy had a fight. He wanted to make her mad." She touched Sue's arm. "Don't expect him to—to even talk to you Monday. He's like that."

Sue tried to block Cathy's words from her mind. She was probably right. She usually was. The Crowd was noted for its ability to cut anyone not a part of the group. Sue slipped into the front seat beside Dad quietly. She could dream for a little while, couldn't she? Dave—the Peppermint Prom— and the pink dress. She smoothed the full skirt gently. *Thank you, pink dress,* she said under her breath.

2

The New Crowd

SUE NEVER KNEW A weekend could drag so. In spite of Cathy's warning, she'd hoped Dave would phone. But although the dear little instrument of communication almost jangled itself off the table with calls for Mom, Dad, and even Jay, it didn't give a buzz for her. Still, she was glad for the usual Saturday chores of scrubbing the bathroom and cleaning her bedroom, because they kept her in the house on a chance that Dave might call. She felt a little bit like dying when Mom sent her to the store for milk. And sure enough, even though she made the trip in record time, when she turned up the walk to her home she saw Mom at the window, gesturing for her to hurry.

Sue hurried, all right. She hurried so much she almost fell into the house.

"Telephone," Mom said with an odd look in her eyes. And Sue knew it was Dave.

"Hello," she said. And her voice trembled.

"Hi." It was Cathy.

"Oh, you." She couldn't keep the disappointment from her voice.

"Sure, me." Cathy sounded cheerful. "Who'd you expect, the President?" Sue heard Cathy chuckle. "Oh no. You didn't think it was Dave, did you?"

"What do you want?" Sue's flare of resentment at Cathy's words made her voice sound almost rude.

"Mom gave me a dollar for washing windows." Cathy's voice was smooth and unhurried. "I wanted you to go to the Avenue to buy a record."

"Can't. I've too much to do."

"Please."

"Huh-uh. But bring the record by and we'll play it."

"Okay." Cathy sounded resigned as she hung up the receiver.

By the time Cathy came with the record, Sue wished she'd gone along for the walk. Dave still hadn't called. Today was such a letdown after last night. Never again, probably, would she have so much fun as she had last night.

"We'll go in the playroom to listen." Sue reached in the cooler for the crackers and peanut butter. "Get some milk out of the refrig, Cathy."

The girls sprawled out on the rug and listened to the new piece. It was the hit of the week. The orchestra had played it several times last night, and Sue felt almost like crying as Cathy played it over and over. She hardly heard Cathy's constant chatter.

"Look," said Cathy, taking off the record and slipping it into its case. "I'm going home. You don't even listen to me. I asked you if you think we'll make traffic squad next time, and all you said was 'mmmmmm.'"

Sue raised startled eyes. "I'm sorry. I must have been asleep or something."

"No, you weren't. You were thinking of that darned Dave. Don't you know he won't even give you a tumble? He's just out of our league. He won't even know you're alive on Monday."

"Maybe not," Sue admitted. "But he did know I was there last night"

"Sure, sure." Cathy's brown eyes flashed. "But just to make Judy mad. It was an accident he picked on you. Anyone would have done."

Sue was glad Cathy left. A few more remarks like that and she wouldn't feel able to live through the day. Cathy could be right, though. Dave probably had picked her by accident. What if he'd chosen Cathy instead? She was cute and little with real golden-colored hair, and *no freckles*. In fact, when you came right down to it, she would have been a better choice. The more you thought about it, it was sort of surprising Cathy wasn't in The Crowd.

Ellen, now—Sue couldn't see Dave picking Ellen no matter what. Ellen was chunky. "Solidly built," as Dad said. Someday, Mom prophesied, Ellen would be a beauty. Right now she was just—Ellen. Good-natured, jolly, a follow-the-leader girl. Cathy could cut you down to size, but Ellen gave you a build-up.

At supper Sue managed to put away a good meal in spite of her melancholy mood. She was glad when Mom and Dad decided on a movie and left her to sit with Jay and Kit. She read them their favorite stories three times apiece, and after putting them to bed she gave herself up to an evening of listening to the hit tunes on the radio—and reminiscing.

Sunday morning she was glad to put away her dream of Dave ever calling, and was even enthusiastic when Mom and Dad suggested a picnic at the beach after Sunday school. She had fun making sand castles and digging wading pools for Jay and Kit. It was fun, too, collecting sea shells and watching the sand crabs bury themselves in the wet sand. Fun—and for the first time since the Peppermint Prom she felt like herself again. Wouldn't Dave's eyebrows raise if he could see his dancing partner jumping rope with a long piece of seaweed!

After a lunch with the minimum of sand in the sandwiches, Sue took Jay for a ride on the roller coaster. Then she and Dad tried their luck at a baseball throw. Sue's throwing arm must have been in good form, because she won a choice of prizes—and picked a tiny mother-of-pearl harmonica that she fastened onto her purse as a charm.

Now—too soon—it was Monday and time to go to early morning orchestra rehearsal. It was time, too, to take extra pains with her clothes. There wasn't a wrinkle in her skirt, and the blue blouse, the mirror told her, brought out the blue in her eyes. She'd been saving this blouse for a special occasion. Maybe today was it. If only the sun at the beach hadn't brought out all those freckles!

"Hurry right home," Mom said as Sue picked up her lunch. "I've an appointment at the dentist and need you to take care of Jay and Kit."

"I will." Sue felt loaded down as she did every orchestra morning with her violin case and stack of books. She was glad that she was walking to school alone today—Cathy and Ellen weren't in orchestra. She could sort out her thoughts and plan her actions. Should she be cool and aloof, or gay and friendly? If Dave didn't talk to her, should she drop a book or something? No, that would be too corny. Better just drift with the day. She shifted her books and violin to a more comfortable position as she climbed the hill to Taft. Once in orchestra there was no time for any more plans.

First recess arrived, and she was still full of indecision as she moved with the stream of students flowing down the ramp to the playground. If only Cathy and Ellen were in her class. Not that she didn't like the kids in nine-three, but she'd been going to school with the two girls since kindergarten, and there was something awfully nice about the old and the familiar. Maybe that's why students were separated from former classmates when they came to Taft Junior High, so that the kids who "graduated" from the town's six-year schools would mix and make new friends.

"Has his royal highness spoken?" Cathy asked her as soon as they met in the yard.

"He's over there," Ellen said.

Sue turned her back deliberately toward the direction to which Ellen pointed. "Don't," she begged. "Don't let him know we even see him." In desperation she turned attention to her purse. "Look," she said. "See the cute harmonica charm I won at the beach." Her voice sounded loud even to her own ears. If only recess were over.

At noontime, Sue took her lunch out into the yard with dread and anticipation. Dave hadn't talked to her, but recess was so short. Now there was an hour. Surely—surely he'd at least say. "Hi." She sat on the low wall with Cathy and Ellen, and they spread open their sandwich bags on their laps. This was their favorite lunch place, and one they usually had to themselves. Sue followed Cathy's surprised eyes and saw Laura, Judy's best friend, and some of the other girls in The Crowd coming toward them.

Laura stopped squarely in front of Sue. "Guess you thought you were something Friday," she started without any preliminaries. "Just thought I'd tell you Dave and Judy will be going steady again by tonight."

Sue felt her face flush as anger rose in her throat. "So?"

"So you don't need to bother with wearing new blouses. He won't even see you." Laura turned on her heel and walked away, the other girls following her.

Sue felt the tears sting her eyes. "That—that——" she sputtered, too angry to get the words out.

"Judy's scared," Cathy said flatly. "She's afraid she won't be going steady with Dave by tonight. That's why she sent Laura."

"Isn't it exciting?" piped Ellen. "For a minute I thought you were going to slap Laura."

For a minute there, Sue had thought so too. Cathy could be right. Maybe Judy *was* scared. Maybe Dave hadn't spoken to *her* today, either. She glanced around the yard quickly. No. There they were. Judy and Dave. And they looked awfully chummy. Dave wouldn't "even see her." Laura had no reason to be so nasty. Right now Sue wished she were home. And she had the whole afternoon to live through.

In math class, the minutes ticked by even slower than they had at the dance before she met Dave. They weren't like rubber bands stretching, but like inchworms. Finally dismissal bell rang. Sue didn't stop to talk to anyone. She gathered up her books and hurried to the orchestra locker for her violin. Waiting on the steps of the auditorium were Ricky and Chester. Today was Cathy and Ellen's make-up sewing lesson. She had never known the boys to look so good. The safe, the familiar, the known.

"I'll take your books," offered Ricky. "Hear you were quite the girl Friday night. Didn't even miss me."

Sue handed over her books. "Sure I did. Everybody did," she said glibly.

Ricky, she discovered as they started down the hill, was in a talkative mood. His brother had brought him a new microscope lens. He'd made some new slides. Near the bottom of the hill Sue saw a figure that made her heart do a flip-flop. Dave—alone. Would he speak? They had to walk right by him.

He stepped out into the middle of the sidewalk, blocking their way. "I'll walk you," he told Sue.

"But—I'm with——"

"These guys don't mind, do you?" Dave looked squarely at Ricky and Chester.

"Gotta hurry," Chester said, slipping past and breaking out into almost a run.

"It's up to you, Sue," Ricky said.

"Okay, Sue, let's go," Dave demanded.

Sue was never quite sure what her answer would have been if she hadn't seen Judy and Laura at that moment, watching them from across the street. "Okay," she said, reaching for her books.

"He'll take 'em. And this too." Dave took the violin case out of Sue's grasp and passed it to Ricky. "Leave them at her house," he ordered.

Sue dropped her hands to her side as she looked helplessly from Dave to Ricky. Ricky's eyes looked angry and his face flushed. He caught Sue's glance and smiled briefly. "Okay with me, Sue," he said. He walked off, leaving Dave and Sue standing at the corner.

"We'll go have a lemonade," Dave announced. "Come on. Let's rush it."

Last week, if she'd dreamed of walking home from school with Dave, Sue would have been thrilled. Now there was something not quite right with the picture. Dave had talked to Ricky just as Laura had spoken to her. "You know," she said. "You—you—I mean I—I——"

"You know," Dave interrupted. "You're going to be a good stutterer."

"I don't usually stutter," Sue flared. "It's just that you were so rude."

"To those creeps?" Dave sounded astonished.

"They aren't creeps," Sue protested. "They're my friends."

"Oh, come on, let's not fight. Be nice." Dave reached for her hand. "Maybe you better have straight syrup instead of a lemonade, to sweeten you up."

Be nice. Don't fight Orders, orders. Dave was good at them. Oh well, maybe she should just enjoy herself. She could apologize to Ricky later.

The creamery looked as though not another kid could squeeze in when Dave opened the door and elbowed his way through the crowd. The jukebox was blaring, and the laughing and talking of the kids reminded her of the noise at the dance.

"Hi." Dave greeted first this person and then that, and in the back booth some of his friends moved over so they could have a seat. Sue sat down stiffly.

"Make it two lemonades," Dave shouted over the din. He leaned back and stretched his legs out under the table. "Relax," he told her.

And she was just beginning to when she saw Judy and Laura slip out from another booth and approach them.

"Hi, Dave," they greeted in unison. Laura's glance slid over to her, then drifted to another girl in their booth. "Hi, Maxine," she greeted the other girl pointedly.

Sue felt Judy's appraising look. "Cute blouse," Judy said. "I saw it on the bargain table at the Style Shoppe."

"You did?" Sue opened her eyes wide in feigned amazement. "Mom made it."

Whatever answer Judy might have given, Dave thwarted. "Hey," he called, waving his arm. "Hey, George, Mo, where you characters been?"

The two boys wove their way over to the table. George was the one who had warned her. Sue flushed under his gaze. She looked up at Mo. She'd known him from way back—third grade, in fact. And he'd been leader of The Crowd at Taft—until Dave transferred. Sue never could see why. Back in the lower grades his pranks had always been so mean, but he was big stuff at Taft.

"Hmmmm," Mo sneered. "Look who's out of her league." He turned to Judy and Laura. "Come on, kids. George and I'll treat you Cokes."

Dave was busy with his lemonade and paid no attention to the four leaving. The other kids in the booth went on with their conversation as though there'd been no interruption. Sue sipped thoughtfully at her straw. Judy was darling-looking, and she had beautiful clothes. She had the kind of figure, too, that set them off. Not tiny like Cathy, not tall like Sue. A just-right size. Her blue-black hair fell in soft, natural waves to her shoulders. Her full lips were colored a brighter red than Sue was ever permitted to use. It gave her added glamour. Absolutely perfect-looking, Sue concluded, if it weren't for her eyes. Not just because they were close together, but because of a hard, calculating look. Before Dave came to Taft, Judy had been Mo's girl. That's the way it was. Judy always went with whoever was on top.

She glanced over at Maxine. Did she, too, resent Sue's intrusion into The Crowd? Maxine smiled across at her.

"That *is* a cute blouse," she said. "You're lucky your mom can sew."

"Cute kid." Dave patted Sue's hand, and she could feel the color surge to her face. "Come on, let's shove off."

Dave angled his long legs out of the booth and Sue followed. Out on the sidewalk, she felt quite at ease with her hand in Dave's. But there was something she should settle right now. She took a deep breath. "Look, Dave," she started. "Don't you think you've carried this far enough?"

"What?"

"Using me to make Judy mad."

"Let her burn. It's good for her."

Let her burn? Sure, that was fine—if Judy was the only one to get burned. Sue felt like a pawn in one of Dad's chess games.

At the corner, half a block from her home, Dave stopped. "End of the line," he said.

Sue felt momentary resentment. When a boy walked you home, he usually took you right to the front door, didn't he? She looked at Dave. Apparently this was ordinary procedure for him. "Okay," she said. "See you." She started down the block.

"Hey, Sue."

She stopped and turned.

"Phone me tonight." Dave raised his hand in a salute, then loped across the street.

Well! Of all the nerve. Girls didn't phone boys, according to the code at her house. Not if Mom or Dad had anything to say about it. With a rueful grin she hurried on home.

"Hi, Mom," she called as she opened the front door. "Guess what?"

She spotted her books and violin on a chair. "Hi, Mom," she called again. Then with a flash of remembering, she knew Mom wasn't home. There was that dental appointment. Mom took Jay and Kit to the dentist with her? Oh no! Sue sighed. Now she was really in for it!

3

Family Council

SUE GRABBED UP HER books and violin and hurried to her room. She'd change, set the table for supper, and get started on her practicing. Maybe, then, Mom wouldn't be too angry. But taking those two live wires, Jay and Kit, to the dentist would be no picnic. Mom would probably come home more crisped than when she left. Oh well, might as well try. She slipped quickly into shirt and jeans and remembered to hang up her blouse and skirt. When she got down to the kitchen she saw the note. It was just one word printed in blue crayon on one of those cardboards the laundry put in Dad's shirts. Mom usually saved them for Jay's and Kit's scribbling. "THANKS," the card said. Just that. "THANKS." Mom was mad.

As she set the table, Sue worried over what Mom would say. At least she'd make sure the table was completely set so there'd be no "where are's" during the meal. After a double check, she raced up the stairs to start her practicing. A half dozen times through on her finger exercises and she had them down pat. There was something about the last exercise that reminded her of the fast numbers at the Peppermint Prom. Slowly, cautiously her fingers found the notes of the newest hit tune. She played it faster, more surely the second time through, and then—and then—she really whizzed through it. Pretty good, even if she did think so herself. That piece would always remind her, most likely, of the Peppermint Prom—and Dave Young.

"Well!"

Sue dropped her bow she was so startled. "Mom, oh, Mom." She jumped up, almost knocking the music stand over. "I'm sorry I forgot. Honest."

The left side of Mom's face looked stiff as she smiled at Sue. "It was a pretty serious bit of forgetting, Sue."

"Were they just terrible?" Sue looked at Kit and Jay as they crowded past Mom into her room.

"I don't know." Mom turned to Jay and Kit. "Were you?"

"Ricky said we were good, very good," Jay announced. "Huh, Kit?"

"Ricky?" Sometimes, Sue decided, Jay and Kit didn't make sense.

"Pick up your bow, Sue." Mom sounded serious. "I was angry with you, quite angry, when Ricky and Chester brought your books and violin by and said you'd gone off with Dave. And when Chester said they had to carry your things home or Dave would have beaten them up, I almost exploded."

"Beat them up? Chester is stupid!" Sue was indignant. "Dave wasn't too polite, maybe, but *beat him up?* Chester gives me a pain."

"Calm down, Sue. Remember I'm the one who has reason to be angry."

Sue forced herself to relax.

"Anyway, Ricky said you'd probably stop at the creamery, and I was going to stop by there and pick you up when he volunteered to take charge of Kit and Jay."

"He's good, too," interrupted Jay.

"He told us stories about bugs," Kit added.

"So this time Ricky saved the day for one Miss Stevens," Mom concluded. "Now you go on with your practicing, and Jay and Kit can help me with dinner."

As Mom went down the stairs, trailed by the young generation, Sue just sat and stared at her music. What if Mom had come into the creamery and made her leave? What a horrible thought! She certainly owed Ricky a vote of thanks. Funny, when you expected a good scolding you got nothing. And other times. . . . Well, Mom was being sweet. And Ricky—she'd thank him tomorrow at school.

One of the house rules at the Stevens' home was that Sue made or received no phone calls until her homework was completed. Supper over, the table cleared, and the dishes done, she settled down at the dining-room table with her civics book before her. Mr. Henderson had announced a quiz for tomorrow. And he'd given the class a long list of names they were to be able to identify. Long? There were thirty-five names. She wondered if she'd ever get through. *Daniel Boone, Meriwether Lewis, Davy Crockett.* Now if it were only Dave Young! Good-looking, tall, brown hair, blue eyes, the kind of shoulders that would put him on the junior varsity football squad next year at Claramar High, arrogant . . . *"phone me."* If only she could. But Mom and Dad would blow a fuse if she did. Better stick to Davy Crockett . . . James Madison . . . Zachary Taylor . . . she recalled that talk a couple of years ago.

Mom had come storming home from a PTA meeting. "Honestly," she'd said. "Those mothers make me boil. Two of them bragged—*bragged,* mind you—that their sons can scarcely get their homework done, what with all the phone calls from girls."

"What girl would phone a boy?" Dad snorted.

"But they do, Mom," Sue said. "Ellen's big sister does lots."

"It won't happen here." Mom was emphatic. "It's just not done."

"That's just old-fashioned," Sue protested.

"Oh no it isn't, young lady," Dad boomed. "A boy does

the pursuing, and don't forget it. It cheapens a girl, calling up boys."

So Sue had promised she wouldn't ever, ever phone a boy. Now she struggled with that promise. It would be so easy to look up the number—to dial. Mom and Dad wouldn't even have to know. But a promise was a promise. *Brigham Young . . . Kit Carson . . .* Sue worked on and on. Some she knew, some she didn't. And the textbook had an annoying way of skipping around that made looking them up difficult. She'd just about reached the end of the list when the phone rang.

"It's for you." Mom looked puzzled.

Sue's heart was pounding as she took the phone. "Hello."

"Hi, Sue," Sue's hopes dropped. "This is Maxine."

"Oh, hi."

"Dave told me to give you his phone number. You're to call him."

" I—I can't."

"You'd better. Dave said to."

"I can't," Sue repeated. House rules were so difficult to explain. "My parents won't let me."

"Won't let you phone Dave?"

"Any boy. It's a rule."

Maxine whistled. "Golly, your parents sure are peculiar."

"They are not." Sue found herself defending them. "Girls just shouldn't call boys."

"How do you think I know Dave wants you to call?" Maxine asked.

"He could dial, couldn't he?"

"Dave? Dave Young? He doesn't have to."

"And neither do I." Sue put the phone back in its cradle angrily. She saw Mom regarding her with a strange expression.

"What was that all about?" Mom asked.

"Maxine—she's in Ellen's class—told me to call Dave."

"The boy who took you for a lemonade—the one who danced with you at the Peppermint Prom?"

Sue nodded.

"The one Chester says would beat him up if he didn't take orders." Mom made the statement flatly, disapproval in her eyes.

"Chester, Chester, Chester. He's always thinking up stuff."

"Just like his mother." Mom patted Sue's shoulder. "I was forgetting. Come on in the living room if you're through your homework. Relax."

Relax. She was beginning to hate the word. "I've just one more name, Mom." Sue flipped over the pages in the book, then made a final scribbling note. She stood up and stretched. Golly, it was good to be finished after leaning over a book for so long. She flopped down beside Dad on the davenport.

He put his arm around her and drew her close. "Did *the*

boy talk to you today?" His voice was loving and gentle and teasing all at the same time.

"Uh-huh." She leaned her head against his shoulder. "Oh, Dad, he's cute. Really he is. I think maybe you were sort of like him in the olden days."

"Wait a minute," Dad protested. "Olden days—I've still got my own teeth."

"Oh, Dad, you know what I mean." She struggled herself upright. "But he is cute."

"Good taste, too, picking my chick."

"Oh, that" Sue's eyes clouded. "He didn't pick me because he liked me—just to make Judy mad."

"And who's this Judy?"

"The girl he went steady with. They're in The Crowd."

"The Crowd?"

"You know, Dad, the best crowd at school." Her words tumbled over each other as she tried to explain. "It's like—it's like a layer cake, I guess. The crowds at school, I mean. There's the bottom layer—they're the drips. You know. The Mamas' babies, the kids who never do anything. Then there's the second layer. I guess Cathy and Ellen and I are in there. We're the biggest group. We take part in school activities and all that, and we have fun. It's pretty good, being the second layer. But the top! That's the one with the icing. The elite. They're *in,* and they know all the other kids would like to be *in,* too."

"The school officers," Dad agreed.

"No. You need citizenship and scholarship grades to be president and stuff. But they have the best parties. They start the newest fads."

"Uh—this Dave. What is his last name?" Dad's voice took on a doubtful tone.

"Dave Young."

"He isn't the one Mrs. Cannon told me about, is he?" Mom broke in.

Mrs. Cannon? The block gossip? "I—I don't know."

"Was he suspended from school recently because of throwing things?"

"Uh-huh." Sue giggled. "He threw a milk carton over one of the rafters—and it hit Mr. Mack. The trouble was, it was full."

"That's funny?" Dad's voice was stern.

"Not really," Sue admitted. "But the principal sure looked odd with milk dripping all over him."

"Young lady." Dad's voice was deadly serious now. "I think you'd better leave well enough alone. You're not the type for The Crowd."

"You mean I'm not good enough to have the icing?" There was a tearful note in Sue's voice. "You mean I'm just ordinary, just middle-middle."

"Not at all." Dad took her hand. "You compared the social strata to a layer cake. But remember, the batter is all the same. It's just chance which layer is on top."

"No, it isn't," Sue argued. "Mom saves the smoothest layer for the top. And The Crowd at school is real smooth."

"Susan Stevens!" Mom interrupted. "I'm disappointed. I thought you'd learned by now you don't judge people by how *smooth* they are, but for *what* they are."

"Then—if Dave wants to walk me home again, he can't."

"I won't say he can't," Dad said quietly. "Just that I'd rather you didn't want him to."

Not want him to? Sue could hardly believe her ears. Not want Dave Young to walk you home from school?

"In any case," Mom put in, "you won't have to worry about it tomorrow. I'm picking you up for a booster shot."

And Wednesday the school Welfare Club was going to stuff Easter seal envelopes. And Thursday was violin. And Friday . . . oh, what was the use? By Friday, Dave and Judy would be going steady again for sure. Sue drew herself up from the davenport. "Good night," she said. "I'm going to study."

"Sue, dear, aren't you going to kiss us good night?" Dad's voice sounded tender again. She longed to throw herself into his arms as she used to do when she was little and skinned her knee or banged her shins. But she walked across the room cool and dignified, and the kisses she gave were as detached as she could make them.

"Darling," Mom pleaded. "We just don't want you hurt."

"You think I'm middle-middle." Sue kept her voice hard so the tears wouldn't show.

In the sanctity of her bedroom, Sue turned on the radio. She blinked back the tears as she set her hair. Then she crawled into bed with her civics list. But it was hard to concentrate. Middle-layer. Ordinary. It hurt when your parents thought you were *that*. Everything was getting so muddled and mixed up. The ten o'clock news came on. She switched off the radio. Mom and Dad were usually so swell. Maybe they were really only trying to help. Maybe she should go down and kiss and make up.

She slipped out of bed and was at the top step when she heard the phone ring. Dad answered, started to say something, and then she heard the phone slammed down.

"Insufferable pup," he thundered. "Hung up without even leaving his name when I said Sue was in bed."

Sue tiptoed back to her room. Now was no time to make up. Dad was really angry. She got back into bed and switched off the light. Daniel Boone, Kit Carson, Davy Crockett . . . *Dave Young—he'd phoned*. She hugged the thought to her as she drifted off to sleep.

4
After School

SUE MADE PEACE WITH Mom and Dad at breakfast. Dave was kept scrupulously out of the table talk. Dad didn't even mention the phone call—and she was glad. Jay and Kit barely finished their fruit juice and cereal before they were out in the back yard with jars in hand on a pre-school hunt for caterpillars and bugs. Ricky had started something with his nature talk. Sue gave Mom and Dad an extra special good-by kiss. "I love you, really I do," she told them as she picked up her books. She hurried out to meet Cathy and Ellen at the appointed corner.

Sue almost reached the end of the block when she saw Mrs. Cannon in her garden. She quickened her steps and looked the other way. If she could only just get past . . .

"Good morning, Sue," called Mrs. Cannon. "Come see my tulips."

If she could pretend she didn't hear . . . but Mrs. Cannon's voice was as penetrating as a drill. She stopped reluctantly.

"My," Mrs. Cannon looked Sue up and down. "My, aren't we the big girl now. Lipstick, too."

"Ninth graders can wear it," Sue said. "Your tulips are very pretty, Mrs. Cannon. And I've got to hurry. My friends won't wait."

"Boy friends?" Mrs. Cannon's smirk hid her eyes in fat wrinkles.

"Cathy and Ellen."

"Hmmmmmm." Mrs. Cannon sounded knowing and doubtful all at the same time. "I thought it might be that rowdy David Young I saw you with yesterday."

Dad always teased Sue about leading with her chin when she got angry. She could feel it thrust forward now as she tensed at Mrs. Cannon's cutting remark. *Rowdy David Young.* Sue struggled to keep her voice civil. "I'll miss my friends," she said. "See you." She fairly ran down the street without waiting for a reply. *Stupid old busybody.* Rowdy Dave Young—big girl Sue. So what if she was tall? The way Mrs. Cannon said it, it sounded like an insult. Grownups had the advantage on remarks, that was for sure. They could say anything personal and get away with it. But if she'd said. "My, Mrs. Cannon, what a big woman. Been putting on weight?" she'd have been considered impudent.

Sue turned the corner just in time to see Ellen and Cathy starting off without her.

"Wait," she yelled.

Cathy and Ellen stopped until she caught up. "That Mrs. Cannon," she stormed. "You're so lucky she doesn't live near you. I hate her."

Cathy laughed. "We all have our Mrs. Cannons," she said with an exaggerated sigh.

"Only mine has frizzy hair and talks to flowers," Ellen added.

"Ours is the worst." Sue refused to be mollified as she went into a fresh tirade on Mrs. Cannon. It wasn't until she was on her way to class that she recalled she hadn't mentioned anything to Cathy and Ellen about Dave and the lemonade and the phone call.

Everything, Sue decided in the days that followed, was the same as B.D. (Before Dave). And why she ever thought it would be any different, she didn't know. Because Dave was certainly no part of her life these days. Except for a brief. "Hi" at noon Tuesday, she hadn't even seen him. The boys were now deep in baseball practice during the noon hours, and she had promised Mr. Henderson she'd paint some murals for Public School Week, so she didn't get out to the field with the other girls to watch the games. But Dave could have phoned, and Sue waited each night for the call that never came.

There was *one* subtle difference, though. It was just that kids who never bothered to talk to her before would say. "Hi." Maxine, especially. Even Judy and Laura must have decided to declare a truce, because they spoke to her too.

After school there had been no chance for Dave to walk home with her. The booster shot, Easter seal envelopes, and violin lesson had seen to that. Now she waited on the auditorium steps for Cathy and Ellen. As it was Friday, they'd make their weekly date to go to the movies.

As she stood there, Sue felt a little like a pack horse. Books, violin, and a big roll of paper for another mural.

Cathy arrived first. "Boy," she exclaimed. "Sure you didn't forget something?"

Sue grinned. "If I did, I wouldn't have another hand to carry it with anyway."

"Now's the time for Chester or Ricky to come by. You could use some help."

"I haven't seen them since Monday." And that was something to puzzle over, Sue thought. Were the two boys avoiding her?

"Hi!" Ellen puffed up breathlessly. "I was scared you might go off without me. Mrs. Robins wanted to talk to me about my talking and she did the talking and . . ." Ellen paused for breath. "Why all that stuff?" She nodded toward the conglomeration in Sue's arms.

"Another mural," Cathy explained for Sue. "Glad our home room is doing geometrical designs."

"My dad's turn to drive us to the show," Ellen stated.

"Same time," said Cathy.

"Same station," added Sue. That was the nice thing about having friends. Going to the show on Fridays was expected, with no troublesome arranging to do. It was as matter of fact as peanut butter and jelly sandwiches. "Let's get going," she added. "All this stuff is killing me."

"Aren't we waiting for Chester and Ricky?" asked Ellen. "They were here yesterday."

"They probably saw Sue's load—and didn't feel like working," Cathy said.

"Fine friends—evading work." Ellen laughed.

"No," said Sue slowly. "They're not evading work. They're evading me." It hurt to put the thought into words, but it felt better to have it out in the open.

"Pooh," snorted Ellen.

"She's right," corrected Cathy. "They are evading her, I bet. Just as The Crowd has evaded us. They only talk to Sue when we're not around."

Leave it to Cathy, the practical one. It was true—The Crowd did speak to her only when she was alone. They snubbed Cathy and Ellen. Sue felt a surge of loyalty for her two friends. "The Crowd will never make any difference to us," she declared. "We're going to be best friends for ever and ever."

Ellen giggled. "You sound like you're taking an oath or something. Of course we'll be best friends. We'll be each other's bridesmaids and godmothers. I mean for each other's children. I mean . . ."

"If we're going to be best friends," Cathy interrupted, "here's our chance, Ellen. Look who's at the corner."

Dave! Sue's heart skipped a beat as she saw him leaning there against the street sign. Would he speak—or ignore her? She tried for nonchalance. "For ever and ever and ever," she heard herself repeat. Dave was looking everywhere but in her direction. He meant to ignore her. She willed herself to walk by—as if she didn't know him. Her step quickened.

"Walk you," Dave said. He stood, blocking her way.

Sue swallowed. *For ever and ever and ever.* "Walk us," she amended.

Dave frowned.

"I'm walking with Cathy and Ellen. Aren't you even going to say 'Hi'?"

Dave shrugged. "Hi," he said in a tone he might use to address a couple of dead fish.

Sue felt as though she were riveted to the sidewalk. Whatever move she made would be the wrong one, she knew.

"Oh, for goodness' sake." Cathy sounded annoyed. She tugged at Ellen's sweater and the girls skirted around Dave and Sue. "Four don't fit on a sidewalk, you know."

Wonderful, practical, save-the-day Cathy. Sue felt almost lightheaded as she and Dave started down the street. She looked at him. "No books?" she asked.

"Over the weekend?" Dave sounded amazed. "*You* must be moving the school."

"Just about." Sue stopped in her tracks. "So what will you take?"

"Huh?"

"What will you carry?"

"I don't lug books."

"Here, then, take my violin."

Dave drew back as if the case might burn him, then reached hastily for Sue's books. "You didn't phone." He made the statement in a flat voice.

Sue looked quickly at her friends. They were maintaining a discreet distance ahead. "Neither did you."

"I told you to."

"Girls don't phone boys."

"Who says?"

"My parents."

"Who's to know?"

"Me. Besides, I don't believe in it either."

"You're an odd one." Dave looked puzzled. "In my house I do what I want. I'm my own boss."

"I'm not. And I'm glad." Sue felt a need to explain. "Maybe—maybe no one is *boss*. Mom and Dad—they're the heads of the house. And they tell Kit and Jay and me things to *help*. We *belong*."

"Belong? Not me! Dad's on the road too much. And my stepmother . . ." Dave gave an ugly laugh.

Sue felt a wave of sympathy. Stepmother? She hadn't known. She tried to think of something to say. Her pity must have shown.

"Don't bother." Dave dismissed the subject. "Your friends . . ."

Cathy and Ellen were standing at the corner. This was where they met and parted every day.

"See you tonight," Cathy remarked.

"Remember. My dad's turn." Ellen grinned at Dave. "The show," she explained archly.

"Okay." Sue wished Ellen wouldn't be so obvious. But she only meant to help.

" 'By." Dave raised his hand to the two girls in a half salute.

"They're nice," Sue commented as she watched the two hurry off.

Dave gave a noncommittal shrug. "Okay, I guess."

They walked on in silence. Would Dave suggest a Coke or something? She hoped he wouldn't because of Mom and Dad. And then she got mad because she knew he wouldn't. He'd be embarrassed about carrying her books. No books had its romantic advantages, though. Holding hands for instance. No one could possibly hold hands with all this paraphernalia. They neared the corner where Dave took his departure Monday. A repeat performance today no doubt. Sue gave a mental shrug. There was some sort of saying. "When in Rome do as they do." She reached for her books. "End of the line," she stated.

"Yeah, I go that way." Dave handed over the books.

"I guess you're just scared." Sue realized she'd spoken her thoughts out loud.

Dave snorted. "Scared? Me? What of?"

"To meet parents—girls' parents."

"Heck, no." Dave's voice was scornful. "It's just . . . Heck, why go out of my way?"

"Oh."

"Scared?" Now Dave's eyes were stormy. "Gimme." He reached for Sue's books, then changed his mind and took the violin case. He walked with a determined stride, and Sue had to lengthen hers to keep up. As they passed Mrs. Cannon's, Sue was careful not to glance toward the house.

At her door she reached for her violin.

Dave withheld it. "Scared?" he asked.

It was Sue's turn to be surprised. She opened the door. "Hi, Mom. I'm home," she called.

Her mother came from the kitchen, wiping her hands on the corner of her apron. "Good," she said. "I wonder if you could . . ." She stopped short when she saw Dave.

"Mom," Sue put in hurriedly. "I'd like you to meet Dave Young. Dave, this is my mother."

Dave placed the violin case carefully by the door and stepped forward, hand outstretched. "I'm glad to meet you, Mrs. Stevens," he said, and he gave her the smile that knocked Taft girls for a loop.

Before she could see Mom's reaction, Jay and Kit tore into the room. "It's Ricky," yelled Jay. Then he, too, stopped short.

"Dave," Sue said. "This is Jay—and here's Kit. Kids, this is Dave Young."

Jay stuffed his hands in his pockets and regarded Dave silently—almost belligerently.

"Do you collect bugs?" Kit asked.

Dave shook his head. "Sorry," he said. "I don't."

"Ricky does. He's in-ter-est-ting." Kit said the four-syllable word slowly.

Sue wished fervently she'd left well enough alone and said good-by to Dave at the corner. The look on his face was strange—one she couldn't interpret.

Mom came to the rescue. "Hurry, youngsters," she said. "I need you in the kitchen." She turned Kit around and gave her a friendly pat on her seat. Jay shrugged from her grasp. "You like my sister?" he asked gravely.

Dave seemed to pull his glance from Kit's retreating figure and turned to Jay. "Yeah," he said with an amused smile.

"She likes Ricky." Jay made the announcement flatly.

"That's enough, young man." Mom grasped Jay firmly by the shoulder and marched him toward the kitchen.

Kit poked her head around the corner. "If you *did* collect bugs, then you would be in-ter-est-ting."

Sue opened her mouth but closed it again when she couldn't think of a thing to say.

"She's cute," Dave commented.

"Sue," Mom called, "if you and Dave would like some milk and cookies . . ."

"Uh, no thanks, Mrs. Stevens. I've got to get going."

Sue opened the front door. If only Dave would get going. Jay and Kit were downright embarrassing. She'd have a talk with Mom about them. "'By, Dave. Thanks for carrying my stuff."

Dave hesitated. "Kit's cute," he repeated. He looked down at Sue. "Uh, I'll be at the show. Meet you in the lobby." He'd resumed his regular flip tone.

As she closed the door behind him, Sue wondered. Was he ordering her again? Or was this a halfway date?

That night at dinner, Sue braced herself. "Dad," she said. "Dave walked me home today. He met Mom."

"A very pleasant boy, too," Mom put in.

"And, Dad, tonight when Cathy and Ellen and I go to the show . . ."

"As usual," Dad interrupted.

"Well, Dave might be there too."

"So?"

"What if—what if he wants to sit with me?"

"You're going with Cathy and Ellen?"

"Yes."

"You'll be with Cathy and Ellen?"

Sue's shoulders sagged. "Yes."

"Then I suggest . . ." Dad paused dramatically. "I suggest," he repeated, "that you take care not to sit in the middle."

"Middle?" Sue repeated stupidly.

"Perhaps 'between' would be a better word." Dad gave Sue a broad, conspiratory wink.

"Oh, Dad." Sue jumped up from the table and gave him a hug. "Dad, you're the best."

"Sure I'm the one you think is the best?" Dad teased.

"Dave's cute, too," Sue admitted. "Isn't he, Mom?"

Mom laughed. "Reasonably so—for a boy his age."

"But he doesn't collect bugs," Kit protested.

"And we like Ricky best," Jay insisted.

"I like everybody best." Sue passed her plate for a piece of apple pie. "Everybody in the whole wide world . . . And I *love* apple pie."

5

Popcorn Brawl

THE USUAL FRIDAY QUEUE had already formed at the box office.

"I'll find out how long the show lasts." Sue jumped from the car, and Cathy and Ellen made a slower exit. "Three hours and forty-five minutes, Mr. Scott," she reported to Ellen's father. Cathy and Ellen were already in line.

Mr. Scott checked his watch. "I'll be back for you at ten-twenty sharp."

Sue joined her friends, who were inching toward the box office. She counted out her money and handed it to Cathy. Last year she still managed to get in on a child's ticket. Now she hadn't a chance.

The queue stretched to the corner. It must be a good picture, Sue reflected, as she noticed many grownups in the line. Usually, Friday was conceded to be kids' night—

teen-agers, that is. She scanned the line. Was Dave really coming? She couldn't see him anywhere, although The Crowd was well represented.

"Hey, wake up. I've got 'em." Cathy waved the tickets at Sue. Still no Dave. The three girls found seats as usual in the tenth row from the back. Years ago—when they went to matinees—they decided that was their favorite row. Now they felt out of place in any other row. Sue searched the audience for Dave's dark crew cut without success. Just then she saw Ricky and Chester coming down the aisle. "Hi," she called.

"Hi." The boys returned the greeting, started to move on, then came over.

"The picture is terrific," announced Ricky. "My brother said so."

"Lots of other people must think so, too. Look at the mob." Chester gave Ricky a shove. "Come on, let's get seats."

Cathy glanced at the vacant seats beside them. "Here's a couple," she ventured.

Sue saw Ricky hesitate. She'd often thought that if Ricky ever took time out to have a girl friend, he'd pick Cathy. "Well, maybe," he said.

"Come on." Chester plucked at Ricky's sweater. "Further down for us. Can't see good way back here."

Ricky let himself be pushed forward. "See ya," he called over his shoulder.

"Well," said Cathy with a shrug. "That's the first time I've known them to be so nearsighted."

Ellen giggled. "Chester is just shy. He didn't want us fighting over who sat next to him."

Sue frowned. More evading? Or was this a snub directed at her? They seemed Chester-inspired. She puzzled over it as the theater darkened and the picture started.

For the next couple of hours the girls watched almost motionless. The picture was a thriller and built up such tension that when the man with the gun came unexpectedly into view, Ellen yelled "Look out!" and Sue found her own hand covering her mouth to stifle a scream.

When the picture ended and the lights came on for intermission, Sue felt emotionally exhausted. She sat still while the aisle filled with kids surging out for popcorn and candy.

"Hey, Sue," said Ellen. "Your turn tonight for getting the popcorn. You'd better hurry or the next picture will start before you get back."

Sue found the kids four-deep around the candy and popcorn stand in the lobby. The noise they made was tremendous. She didn't feel ready to become a part of the pushing mob—the picture had been really terrific. The sad part—did her eyes show she'd been crying? She furtively wiped them with the back of her hand.

"Say, Sue."

She was startled by a hand on her shoulder. She spun around. Dave.

"I've been looking for ya." Dave proffered his bag of popcorn. "Where you sitting?"

"With Cathy and Ellen." Sue scooped a couple of pieces of popcorn out of the bag and popped them into her mouth. "I'm supposed to be buying that stuff for us."

"Here, hold this and I'll get them for you." Dave handed her the bag and she gave him the money. "Three bags full," she said—and giggled. Like the black sheep, she thought. But Dave was apparently not up on his nursery rhymes, because he didn't even crack a smile. Sue watched him start to plow through the mob. Then it just seemed to part and let him through. In a minute he was back.

"Okay, lead the way," he said. "I'll carry 'em."

Latecomers were still filing in as Dave followed Sue down the aisle. Cathy was standing by her seat, fuming at a stout woman who was moving into the row.

"This seat's taken," Sue heard her say. "My girl friend went out for popcorn. It's taken."

The woman picked up Sue's jacket and handed it to Cathy. "That's right," she said. "It is taken—by me."

Ellen gave a nervous giggle. "But where will Sue sit?" she asked. "She was with us."

The woman didn't bother to answer. "Come, Henry, this is fine," she said to the little man beside her.

"Here she is now," Cathy protested, pointing across the woman to Sue. "I keep telling her it's your seat," she explained.

"First come, first served," said the woman. "There are no reserved seats here." She settled herself with the finality of a tombstone.

Sue started to protest when she caught Dave's amused grin.

"Sit with ya," Dave said, and his grin grew broader.

"Here." Sue took two bags of popcorn and passed them to Cathy and Ellen. She took her jacket in exchange. "Sit with *you*," she amended. "Wait for me—for sure," she told Cathy and Ellen.

She shot a withering look at the woman and man, then felt a little guilty about that look as she followed Dave down the aisle. Because she really wasn't too unhappy about not sitting with Cathy and Ellen. In fact, sitting with just Dave would be much better. She noted with almost a smirk that Judy and Laura were in the row where Dave found a couple of seats. As she scrambled over the half dozen pairs of legs into the vacant seat, she looked back to make sure Cathy and Ellen saw where she was. She waved briefly, then settled into the seat next to Dave's as the theater darkened and the newsreel came on.

Sue munched her popcorn slowly during the news and the cartoon. Then the second feature started, and she leaned back to enjoy it. Dave put his arm across her shoulder, but she shifted her position and he settled for holding her hand.

"How's the cutie?" he whispered, and Sue was glad it was dark so he couldn't see her blush at the compliment. She couldn't think of an answer, not a flip one, anyway. "Did she find any good bugs yet?" he asked.

Sue realized with a pang that he was talking about Kit. "Shhh," she whispered. "Watch the picture."

Dave turned his attention to the screen briefly, then whispered. "Lousy picture."

Was it ever! This was not merely a B picture, it was a D-for-dull picture. She could sense the restlessness of the audience—the general shifting in seats, whispering that became audible, giggling.

She felt something hit her neck and reached back and pulled a piece of popcorn out of her collar. Another hit her—then another. Soon popcorn was flying all around the theater. Dave's hand went to the back of his neck as it hit him—then suddenly stood, turned, scooped a handful out of his bag, and hurled it back across the rows.

"Don't. Sit down," hissed Sue. The adults behind them muttered angrily, warning Dave to stop. But he took another handful and flung it back deliberately.

The whole theater seemed caught in a deluge of popcorn, and then a woman's scream burst out above the din.

A wave of raucous laughter almost drowned out her words. "I'm wet," she sputtered. "I'm soaked."

"Somebody threw a water balloon," Dave said. He looked back. "Here comes another one!" he warned.

Sue saw a blue balloon wabbling toward them just in time to duck under it. The balloon splatted on the head of a man in front of them, splashing some of the water back on Sue.

The theater was suddenly flooded with light, and Sue watched wide-eyed as the ushers and two policemen strode purposefully down the aisles. They stopped at row after row, motioning for youngsters to get out. They'd just passed her row when the man behind them spoke up. "He's one," he said. "I saw him myself. That one with the crew cut."

The police motioned Dave to the aisle and told Sue to follow. They were herded toward the lobby, and Sue's knees shook so hard she could hardly walk. She looked frantically for Cathy and Ellen. They stared at her in widemouthed disbelief. Now what? Dave was ahead of her. His back had a sort of insolent slouch, and he was walking with deliberate slowness. He shook off the hand of the usher who tried to hurry him along. And then they were in the lobby with the manager, wild-eyed and red-faced, bellowing at them. "Get out," he ordered, and his voice cracked with his rage. "Get out, you bums, and don't come back—ever."

Sue felt herself being pushed toward the exit along with the others. She was scared, scared clear through. This couldn't be happening—not to her. Not being kicked out of a show. Only hoodlums and delinquents were thrown out of places. She couldn't go. Cathy and Ellen . . . Mr. Scott . . . she broke away and approached the manager.

"Please, sir," she said as she tugged gently on his coat sleeve, "please, sir, I can't go. My friends are still here."

The manager brushed her hand away, his face livid. "Friends, you say. You mean we missed a couple trouble-makers? Show them to us."

"No, sir, they aren't troublemakers," Sue tried to explain. "They're my girl friends—and they—they didn't have anything to do with the trouble."

"Where are they sitting?"

"Tenth row from the back." Sue said the words in almost a whisper. They—Cathy and Ellen—couldn't be blamed for anything, could they?

The manager looked doubtful. "Didn't know we had rowdies back there."

Sue felt the color mount to her face. "I—I wasn't with them. I was——"

"She sat with me." Dave was at her side.

"So." The manager's voice was a sneer. "You come with a couple of friends, drop them for a hoodlum, cause a riot, and expect me to let you in again?"

"But I didn't," Sue protested. "I didn't do a thing." She tried to keep her voice steady, but tears were very near. "I bought some popcorn and when I went back, this woman had my seat, and I——"

"Trouble?"

Sue felt relief as she saw the policeman stand by the manager. Maybe he'd listen to reason. The lobby was deserted now, except for the four of them.

"I——" Sue started.

"Just a pickup," the manager interrupted, "trying to alibi her way out of trouble." Sue felt dirty inside at the sneer in his voice.

"You—you——"

Sue saw Dave's hands clench. His eyes were blazing as he took a step forward, hand drawn back.

"Easy there, sonny." The policeman grabbed Dave's arm.

The manager's face was contorted with rage. "Get out," he said between clenched teeth. "Get out and stay out—the two of you. You"—he pointed his finger at Dave—"I've had trouble with you before. Get your pickup out of here."

"Take that back!"

Sue whirled at the new voice. There was Ricky, eyes aflame. "Take it back," he shouted again. "It's like she said. I saw the woman take her seat. What's she supposed to do? Sit in her lap?"

"Get out!" the manager sputtered. "You, too. I run a decent movie house. Get out, the three of you—before I charge you with disturbing the peace."

Sue felt the blood drain from her face. He wouldn't listen. He'd never listen. She turned to the policeman. "My friends," she said desperately. "I've got to tell them first . . ." She stopped, her eyes staring across the lobby. There, at the ladies' dressing-room door, stood Mrs. Cannon. How long had she been there? How much had she heard? This was like a nightmare—a horrible dream. Only she was awake, living it through. Mrs. Cannon caught Sue's glance and came over.

"I'll tell them," she said, and her tone was sugar-sweet. "You were with Cathy and Ellen, weren't you?"

Sue detected a gleam of delight in Mrs. Cannon's eyes. She looked like a cat with a saucerful of cream. Sue nodded—yes, it was Cathy and Ellen she'd come with—how long ago?

"All right, kids, on your way." The policeman guided Dave and Ricky to the door. Sue followed.

"Punks," she heard the manager say. "Delinquents."

"You poor man." Mrs. Cannon was sympathizing. "This modern generation—birds of a feather——"

The door closed behind them, and Sue shivered in the night air. They stood under the bright lights of the marquee. The street was deserted. Dave and Ricky glared at each other in thin-veiled disgust.

"Well, hero," said Dave, "if you hadn't been so nosy, you wouldn't be here."

"And if it weren't for you, she wouldn't be here," said Ricky. "I'll walk you home, Sue."

"I will," stated Dave.

Sue looked from one to the other. Her stomach churned. This was so horrible. She felt so tainted, so humiliated. This was the kind of stuff that got into papers. Dad . . . Mom . . . why hadn't she stayed with Cathy and Ellen? Why was she standing out here? Because of a couple of boys. Boys! She hated the creatures.

"It's up to you, Sue," Ricky said. "Who'll walk you home?"

Sue's humiliation changed to fury. "Walk each other home," she stormed. "I'm going to call my dad."

She turned on her heel and walked with quick steps to the corner drugstore, digging in her pockets for the dime.

6

The Summons

A NEW DAY. A new week. Sue slipped quietly into her seat and listened while Mr. Henderson took the attendance. He closed the book, rose, and walked casually to Sue's desk.

"Here," he said. "Report at recess."

She looked at the slip of paper. This was the first summons Sue had ever received. She was to see Mr. Mack in his office. Students commonly regarded a summons with dread, but she had done nothing to worry about—broken no school regulation.

In fact, now, as she studied the summons, she knew exactly why Mr. Mack wanted her. She'd applied for traffic duty weeks before. This was to tell her when to report—and what corner she would have. She felt tingly with anticipation. How she needed those traffic points for the coveted Block T. Scholarship, citizenship, glee, band, orchestra, after-school sports—they all counted for points. Sue had quite a few accumulated, what with both orchestra and glee. But she needed a half dozen more to be *sure*.

The minutes passed quickly as Sue worked out her algebra. Today's ratios were much easier than the area problems they had to solve with "pi" involved. When the recess bell rang, she was out of her seat before it stopped. She raced down the corridor.

"Hey!" Cathy grabbed Sue's arm. "Where's the fire?"

"Cathy!" Sue beamed. "Just think! Mr. Mack's calling me into his office—to put me on traffic."

"Lucky!" Cathy released her hold. "No wonder you were rushing. All those points!"

When she entered Mr. Mack's office, he was talking on the phone. He motioned her to a chair. Sue sat back and relaxed. This was a moment to enjoy—the appointment would sort of make up for Friday's unpleasantness. But Dad had been swell about picking her up. He even drove Ricky and Dave home. And then, at home in the living room, he'd listened sympathetically to Sue's story. Mom got pretty angry when Sue told how the manager had called her a pickup. But by the time Dad got through explaining the manager's responsibilities—and how he was probably driven to saying things he really didn't mean— Sue felt almost sorry for the man. Almost, but not quite. She couldn't erase the feeling of humiliation she had every time she recalled the ugly scene in the lobby. This appointment was just what she needed—to bolster her self-esteem, and to really please Mom and Dad. Golly, but they were swell people.

"Sue."

She sat up straight. "Yes, Mr. Mack."

"Have you any idea why I've called you to the office?"

Should she play dumb, Sue wondered, or straightforward? Honesty was the best policy. "Yes, Mr. Mack, I do." Sue flashed him her best smile. "I've looked forward to it for so long. It's just exactly what I want to do. All those points, too."

"What?" Mr. Mack looked puzzled. "Do *what*, Sue?"

Sue laughed. Dad had told her she had a bad habit of backing into a subject. That's just what she'd been doing now. "Why, be on traffic, Mr. Mack."

Mr. Mack busied himself with a stack of papers on his desk. He seemed quite intent on having them neat and orderly. He raised his eyes. "Sue," he said slowly, "I'm sorry. You've made a mistake. That traffic assignment is out of the question—now."

"But—but the summons, Mr. Mack." Sue felt a catch in her breath as she forced herself to go on. "What do you mean by—*now*?"

Mr. Mack kept his gaze steady on Sue as his hands fumbled around on his desk, found a paper clip, and began twisting it. He looked as though he wasn't even going to answer. "Sue," he began finally, "I want you to regard us here at school as your friends. We're here to help you—and all the other students."

"I know." Panic caught at her. "I do. I just don't get what you mean by *now*."

"Tell me, Sue"—Mr. Mack pulled his memo pad to him—"were you at the show Friday night?"

Sue could feel her scalp prickle as she dropped her gaze to her lap. "Yes," she managed to say finally.

"Can't you guess, then, what I mean by *now*?"

"You mean because I was—I was——" Sue's voice dropped to a whisper.

"Because you were evicted from the theater, yes." Mr. Mack finished her sentence.

"But—how—why——"

"How did we hear about it?" Mr. Mack's laugh was bitter. "There's not much that goes on around town concerning our students we *don't* hear about." He picked up the paper clip again, and Sue watched it, almost hypnotized, as he contorted it into various shapes. "Here on my desk," he continued, "I have a report from the manager of the theater that several of our students behaved in the manner of hoodlums."

"I'm not a hoodlum," Sue protested hotly. "I didn't do a thing."

"And then," Mr. Mack continued, as if he hadn't heard her, "I received a phone call this morning naming *you* specifically."

"Oh no!" Sue jumped to her feet. "You didn't believe her! You couldn't believe that nosy Mrs. Cannon!"

"I didn't say who phoned, Sue," Mr. Mack said calmly. "And I won't. Please sit down."

Sue sat down again, this time on the edge of the chair. Her cheeks felt fiery. And yet the rest of her felt shivery. She waited for Mr. Mack to go on.

"It's because you've always been one of our better students that I've called you in for a talk," Mr. Mack said. "I just can't see you getting off on the wrong foot after all these months."

"But, Mr. Mack, I didn't *do* anything. Really."

"You mean, Sue Stevens, that you were sitting quietly at the theater, minding your own business—and the usher came down and made you leave?" Mr. Mack's eyebrows showed his disbelief.

"Well, the show was boring, and maybe some of the kids got restless, and——"

"I don't think water-filled balloons can be attributed to just 'restlessness,' do you?"

"Nobody in my row threw balloons."

"What about the popcorn? Do you know anyone who threw that?"

Sue sat silent. Only a squealer would answer that one.

Mr. Mack looked down at his memo pad again. "My notes here," he said, "indicate that two boys were evicted with you. Would you care to tell me who they were?" .

"No." Sue was on her feet. "Why don't you ask that blabber mouth—that Mrs. Cannon? It's what she likes to do."

"Susan Stevens."

Her anger left her as quickly as it had come. She sat down, trying to wipe the clammy feeling from her hands against her skirt. She swallowed hard. "I'm sorry," she said. "Really I am. I didn't mean to be so rude. It's just—just— but the show wasn't even during school time."

"It's time you learned, Sue, that in our community each one of you students is a representative for us as a school, as well as for your own families." Mr. Mack stood up and stuffed his hands in his pockets. "It is you young people," he continued, "who set the reputation of your school. Either you are upstanding citizens or you are delinquents. Your school has either a good name or a bad one."

Sue studied her hands as she folded and unfolded them. Yes, she knew about a school's reputation. Woodlake, in the adjoining suburb, for instance, was supposed to be "good," and Winchester was supposed to be "tough."

"I want us to be friends, as we have been." Mr. Mack paced back and forth across the room. "It seems to me you're at a kind of crossroads, Sue. And for your own good, don't get mixed up with the wrong group. You know as well as I do who the main troublemakers are. You have an outstanding record. Try to keep it."

Sue fought back her tears. Her mouth felt dry—as if it were full of cotton. She couldn't think of words to fill the silence.

"Would you care to tell me your version now, Sue?" Mr. Mack's voice was gentle. "You don't have to, you know. As you say, you weren't on school time."

Mr. Mack's eyes looked almost as kind as Dad's. It would be so easy to tell—to lay the cards on the table, neatly, orderly. Going to the show with Cathy and Ellen as usual. Buying the popcorn, meeting Dave in the lobby . . . the woman taking her seat . . . the stupid second feature . . . the long, unearned walk up the aisle to the lobby where she'd faced the manager . . . she could still see the manager, his face livid . . . and Mrs. Cannon—that Mrs. Cannon!— and Mr. Mack had listened to *her*? Sue swallowed the words that had been on her lips. Mrs. Cannon had sealed her lips.

"I have nothing to say." Sue's words were barely audible.

Mr. Mack sighed. "Well, Sue, that just about closes the matter. You may return to class. But remember, we're here to help."

Sue rose with all the dignity she could muster. She felt so shaken she didn't think she could walk to the door. As she put her hand on the knob, Mr. Mack spoke again. "I suppose I should admire you for your reluctance to involve your friends," he said. "But remember, Sue, this aversion you youngsters have to 'squealing,' as you call it, can have frightening results."

Sue could hardly bring her eyes to meet his. "Thank you," she said, and then wondered what she was thanking him for. Tears blinded her as she stepped out into the corridor. The halls were empty. Classes had already resumed. Sue brushed at her tears. Her cheeks still felt hot. As she approached the ramp leading to her wing, she saw Ricky and Dave. She turned her head quickly, hoping they wouldn't speak—that they'd just leave her alone.

"Say, there." Dave thumped her gently on the shoulder with his fist. "What are you doing out of class?"

"Mr. Mack?" asked Ricky.

She nodded mutely, afraid to trust her voice for fear the tears might show.

"That bad?" persisted Ricky.

"They can't do nothing much," said Dave.

"Anything," Sue corrected automatically. "Have to hurry to class. I'm late." She broke away from the boys and started at a fast pace up the ramp, then glanced over her shoulder. They were just standing there, looking at her. She raised her hand in farewell.

"We're headed for Mack's den ourselves," Dave called. "Nothing to it."

Sue continued on her way. *Nothing to it.* Maybe not—for Dave. At that moment she almost hated him. How could he get Ricky and her involved with Mr. Mack and then say "*nothing to it*"? But in all honesty Dave hadn't involved her deliberately. In fact, she'd involved herself. And none of it—that business at the theater—was really their fault. A stupid picture, an unreasonable manager, a nosy neighbor—so Mr. Mack knew all along who the two boys were. Mrs. Cannon had done her job well.

Sue's steps lagged as she forced herself to return to the classroom. All eyes would be turned on her as she walked in. How she knew it. She straightened her shoulders resolutely. They'd never know—not any of them—what had happened. Not if she could help it. Sue forced a smile as she put her hand on the doorknob.

7

The Closed Door

SUE ENTERED THE CLASSROOM with her smile fixed and frozen. This was like walking a plank or something. She passed one of the boys in Dave's gang. He gave a good-luck salute and winked broadly. She felt her face flush, then managed an answering wink. She slipped quietly into her seat.

"Good news?" the girl across from her whispered. Her gloating look belied her words, as though she knew it was bad. Did other people know why she'd gotten the summons? *Could* they? Sue shrugged, raised her eyebrows elaborately, and opened her Spanish book.

Stalling for time was not easy when the noon bell rang. But Sue was determined. She wanted to leave after the room had cleared out. The boy who had winked came over to her desk.

"Heard about the show," he said. There was admiration in his voice. "Wouldn't you know I wouldn't be there. Must have been something—your dad laying the manager out with one blow." He whistled softly. "Boy, what a deal!"

"Huh?" Sue could only stare her astonishment. Before she could ask what he meant, he'd left. She picked up her lunch and went out to the schoolyard. Ellen and Cathy, sitting over on the stone wall, looked so good. So safe and familiar.

"Did you get it?" Ellen demanded. "Did you?"

"I did, that's for sure." Sue gave a rueful laugh.

"Oh, Sue. You lucky! What corner?"

With a shock, Sue realized Ellen was talking about traffic. "Oh, that?" Sue made her voice as scornful as possible. "You mean *traffic?* Don't be silly."

Ellen frowned. "But I—Cathy said——"

Sue looked at Cathy and remembered that long-ago moment in the hall. "Traffic!" she snorted, giving the word all the scorn she could muster. The resentment and defiance coursed through her like an ugly, consuming thing. "Traffic!" she repeated. "Do you realize what I'd have to give up? Why, I'd never have time for lunch with you, or have fun after school, or . . ." Sue dropped her glance to the ground. *Who was she fooling?* Cathy and Ellen, her two best friends? *Or herself?*

"I'm sorry," she said. "I don't know what's the matter with me. But Mr. Mack didn't give me a traffic job. He bawled me out because of Friday night. Now I'll never get on traffic."

"That's not fair." Cathy sounded indignant. "You didn't do anything."

"Maybe not," Ellen said. "But you should hear the talk. Honestly, you're about the most exciting thing that's happened at Taft for weeks. I heard that your Dad beat up the manager for insulting you. And then I heard that it was Dave who hit the manager. I even heard that you were all taken to the juvenile home, and——"

"Ellen!" Cathy's voice was like a whip.

"Well, they do say that," Ellen persisted. "And that's not all. Some woman called my mother Saturday and said 'Birds of a feather flock together,' and if she knew what was good for me, she'd keep me away from you."

"Ellen!" Cathy's voice was as cold as ice. "Shut up!"

Sue could only stare, wide-eyed. This couldn't be happening. She swallowed twice before she could make her voice work. "You mean," she said slowly, "you mean a woman really did call up your mother?"

"You think I'm a liar?" Ellen seemed to be fired with the subject. "Cathy's, too."

Cathy looked miserable.

"Did she?" Sue demanded. "Did she?"

"Yes." Cathy's voice was low. "At least some woman

started to, but Mom hung up. She won't talk to anonymous callers." She turned to Ellen, her eyes blazing. "I thought we decided not to say *anything*."

Ellen looked sulky. "I wouldn't have said anything if she hadn't been so high and mighty. Besides," she defended herself, "I think it's exciting. I've never gone around with a . . . with a . . ." her voice trailed off into silence.

"Say it," Sue commanded between clenched teeth. "Say it. Were you going to call me a pickup or a juvenile delinquent?"

Cathy stepped forward and put her hand on Sue's arm. "Look," she said. "Don't get so mad. You know how dumb Ellen is about things. She——"

Sue brushed aside Cathy's hand. "Let her talk," she demanded. "Let her have her say." Her glance swept Ellen from head to foot. "Let her get it off her chest—her flat, fat, shapeless chest."

"Sue." Cathy's voice was a plea.

"Go on, talk," Sue insisted.

"Okay." Ellen's cheeks were a fiery red. "My mom said maybe I'd better not pal around with you. You've got too many big ideas."

Sue whirled on Cathy. "And does your mother agree?"

Cathy shook her head. "I told you she wouldn't listen. Besides, she knows you wouldn't do anything *wrong*."

"I guess she knows more than Mr. Mack, then. And all

the rest of them." Sue kept her voice cool, although she was burning with the desire to cry. The hurt inside her was like a raw, open wound.

"Sue," Cathy pleaded. "Don't be like this, please. Ellen didn't mean it. She'll apologize. We don't want you to be hurt. We like you a lot. Really."

Sue fought to control her tears. The sympathy in Cathy's voice . . . She didn't want anyone feeling *sorry* for her—when she'd done nothing. "Well," she said, and her voice sounded ugly to her ears. "I don't like you. I hate you . . . both." She pivoted and went for the rest room at a run. No one . . . no one . . . no one would see her cry. She pushed open the door. A haven . . .

The high pitch of chatter hit her ears. The Crowd—Judy's crowd—they were gathered around the washbasins. As Sue came into view their talk ceased—cut off suddenly as if someone had switched off a radio. And Sue knew they'd been talking about *her.* No haven here. She looked at the lunch bag she still had in her hand, dropped it untouched into the wastebasket, and turned to leave. Where could she go—to be alone? Then, as suddenly as the chatter ceased, it started again. And now the girls were surrounding her.

"Tell us," Maxine asked, slipping her arm through Sue's. "Did Mr. Mack read you the riot act? What really happened Friday?"

"A mouse in disguise," Judy said, but her voice was not

unfriendly. Then, in a slightly warmer tone: "Come join the gang."

Sue looked around the group in wonderment. No scorn here, but a sort of admiration. They seemed to evince a genuine interest. There was an air of camaraderie. They weren't regarding her as a freak—a bad girl. They accepted her—thought her excitingly *one of them*. She felt her tears subside, unused, unneeded. She found herself turning dizzily gay and talkative as she filled in the details. She almost wished Dad had swung on the manager as she dispelled that rumor. Even Judy didn't show any hostility when Dave's name was mentioned. Sue had barely finished her account when the bell rang and the girls picked up their purses to return to class. Just then the door opened and Cathy and Ellen walked in.

"We came to ——" Cathy began.

Sue felt all her shame of the morning sweep back over her. The hurt was open and raw again. She looked around the two girls, over them, then made her way past them to the door, saying nothing until she passed Ellen. Then, with affected politeness, she drew back her skirt. "Sorry," she said, her voice as cold as dry ice, "I didn't mean to *dirty* you." She went out into the corridor, not waiting for anyone.

She was surprised when Maxine caught up with her just as she reached her home room. "Listen," whispered Maxine, her face bright with anticipation. "Judy said maybe I could nominate you for Jay Dee." She hurried off without waiting for a reply.

Sue took her seat thoughtfully. A Jay Dee. That was an exciting new thought. The club that was the most of the most—the inner-sanctum sort of circle. The most exclusive and secret club at Taft. And formed just by Judy and her intimate friends. But why, now, should she suddenly get to be a part of that circle?

For the rest of the school day, Sue paid little attention to her subjects. It was one of those afternoons when the class was working on social studies, so by keeping her binder open and pencil in hand, she was able to retreat behind a kind of wall while she tried to sort out her thoughts.

Her mind was a whirlpool. She tried to go back, step by step, over the whole painful day. The session with Mr. Mack . . . Ellen and her stinging words . . . Cathy, who tried so hard to be peacemaker . . . Maxine and the Jay Dees.

To be honest, perhaps she'd lashed out at Ellen before Ellen started at her. After all, if she were in Ellen's place, she'd be awed and curious if Ellen and Cathy got into trouble. *But she hadn't done anything wrong.* That's what hurt. Sue walked slowly to English.

This business of being hurt, though—it was surely snowballing. She'd been hurt—and in turn hurt Ellen and Cathy. She'd unerringly picked the words that would crush Ellen the most. She knew Ellen detested her figure. Why, oh why, had she called Ellen on her "flat, fat, shapeless chest"? If only she could take the words back. Even apologizing wouldn't erase the words.

What if she *were* asked to be a Jay Dee? Just the idea of having her name put up for the club was stimulating, flattering. Why *would* they ask her? Because of Dave? Or because of the show episode?

That show business! There was a play, Sue recalled, in the bookcase at home. Shakespeare's, she thought, called *Much Ado about Nothing*. And that's just what this was, much ado about nothing. And the person who'd blown up the situation to gigantic size was—that horrible Mrs. Cannon.

Sue sketched a fat face on the corner of her binder paper. She gave it horns and squinty pig eyes. She studied it. A good likeness, she decided, only not as hateful as that woman really was. She slashed across the picture with her pencil. This way, that way. That's what she'd like to do to her *right now*.

"Working hard?"

Sue looked up to see Miss Wilson standing beside her. She instinctively tried to cover the drawing with her hand.

"A she-devil?" Miss Wilson asked.

Sue nodded.

"Hmmmm." Miss Wilson studied the drawing. "You know, we've got one in our neighborhood—just like that," she smiled down at Sue. "But you'd better get on with your school work now, young lady."

Sue flipped the page over and resumed her work. One in every neighborhood? How had Miss Wilson known she was drawing someone she knew? Maybe there was one in every neighborhood—but none was as horrible as her gossipmonger.

When the dismissal bell rang, Sue picked up her books and went straight to the music room for her violin. She wouldn't even look around for Cathy and Ellen. They probably didn't want her around, anyway. She'd go home a different way. She had to think things out.

She walked slowly past the green lawns, the gay flower borders. She stopped and watched some children in a game of hopscotch. Right now she'd like to change places with them. No painful problems, no confusion. Just happy. They simply enjoyed themselves like Jay and Kit did. If she could only undo a little, step back a little, get her life uncomplicated. If only she could erase the whole day and start over.

As the outline of her home came into view Sue knew exactly what she'd do. She'd talk to Mom and Dad about it all after supper. She'd tell them about Cathy and Ellen— how unkind she'd been. She'd tell them about Mr. Mack. And together the three of them would be able to solve the problem. Because that's the way Mom and Dad were— always understanding. Maybe—maybe she wouldn't even wait until tonight. She and Mom could start working things out right now—just as soon as she got in the house.

Sue felt as though her burden had already shifted—grown lighter. She burst through the front door, eager now to start the sharing. She stopped short. There sat Mrs. Cannon—with Mom—in the living room.

"Hello, darling," Mom greeted, giving Sue a brilliant smile. "Come join us in a cup of tea."

Sue forced a smile. "Guess not, Mom. I have loads of homework." She nodded slightly in Mrs. Cannon's direction. "Hello."

Mom laughed. "Come now, Sue. Surely you have time for a brownie. You never pass them up."

Sue shrugged and dropped her books on a chair. She sat down without a word.

"My, what a bright, pretty girl," simpered Mrs. Cannon. "And how was school today?"

She put on a falsely bright smile. "Wonderful," she breathed. "Just super." Was it surprise she saw in Mrs. Cannon's eyes? And why was the woman here today when she so seldom visited?

"Sue really likes school," Mom said as she passed Sue a cup of tea and plate of cookies. "She works so hard. Why, she's almost earned her Block T. And——"

"Where are Kit and Jay?" Sue broke in.

"In the yard." Mom turned back to Mrs. Cannon. "I

suppose I shouldn't say it in front of her, but Sue is a model daughter. We're so pleased with her."

Sue watched Mrs. Cannon as her mother talked. The woman looked back at her with smirking, knowing eyes. She was baiting them, that's what she was doing. Didn't Mom know it? Didn't she remember about the show Friday? Sue realized with a start that Mom didn't know about Mrs. Cannon's being at the theater. Sue had forgotten to tell her.

"Oh, Mom," Sue broke in desperately, "Mrs. Cannon doesn't want to hear this stuff."

"But I do," said Mrs. Cannon. "It's always a delight when parents can be proud of their children. It happens so seldom in this age of juvenile delinquency." She stood up. "But I have to get home to start supper. So——" She walked over to Sue and gave her a pat on the shoulder. "Sue and I are good friends," she simpered, giving Sue a wink. "Why we even have a secret."

Sue felt a blinding rage surge through her. She stood up quickly, almost upsetting the teacup in her hand. "A secret?" she asked, keeping her voice low although she felt like screaming. "About the show, you mean? Mom knows that—and anyway, it's hardly a secret, is it, Mrs. Cannon, after you've told the principal?"

"Sue."

"She means about the show, Mom, Friday night." Sue

kept her eyes on Mrs. Cannon. "She saw me get kicked out—and called Mr. Mack." Sue felt a vindictive pleasure as she saw Mrs. Cannon color.

"Why—why——" Mrs. Cannon sputtered. "That fool."

"Mr. Mack didn't tell me you were the one who called." Sue felt as though she couldn't stop talking now. "He just said a woman did. And you're the only gossipy old busybody who knew—why can't you leave me alone?"

Every inch of Mrs. Cannon's bulky body quivered with rage. "I—why I've never been so grossly insulted in my life." She flounced to the door.

"Sue!" Mom sprang into action. "I insist you——"

"No!" Sue was shouting now. "I won't. I won't say I'm sorry. I'm not. She is a busybody. A fat, snoopy, gossipy old busybody." She turned and fled up the stairs and slammed into her room. She stood there, leaning against the door, breathing hard, almost dizzy with her surging emotions. She could hear faint murmurs at the front door. Then the door closed. She went over and sat on her bed, waiting for Mom's steps on the stairs. Instead, she heard the back screen door slam and the eager, excited voices of Jay and Kit. They bounded up the stairs and burst into her room.

"Look. Fuzzy caterpillars," Jay cried. "We've got three."

"Get out," Sue screamed at them. "Get out. Go away."

Kit and Jay, their eyes startled, their faces scared, backed out the doorway. Sue got up from her bed and slammed the door shut after them. She could hear them tear down the stairs, calling Mom. Sue's hand groped along the top of the door frame for the key that she'd never used. She put it in the hole and locked the door. The tears that had threatened all day long came in a torrent as she threw herself on her bed and buried her head in the pillow. She heard the twisting of the doorknob through her sobs.

"May I come in, Sue?" Mom's voice was calm.

"No. Go away. Please go away."

"Sue, dear, I'd like to talk to you." Mom was insistent.

"No! I want to be alone. Alone, alone, alone." Sue could hear her voice rise hysterically. "Stop picking on me. Just leave me alone."

Sue held her breath, waiting. What would she do if Mom *demanded* she open the door? She heard Mom try the door again—and then her footsteps receded down the hall.

The door! The closed, locked door. Sue eyed it now through her tears. It stood there, a solid symbol. It was a barrier between her and Mom. Between her and the world. It was an insurmountable barrier. Now she couldn't ask Mom and Dad to help. The door was a problem. She was a problem. The world was a problem. She hated the world and the world hated her and she wished she were dead!

8
Steady Does It

BY THE TIME DAD came home from work, Sue was through with her tears. She felt so cried out she thought maybe she'd never cry again. As she exchanged her school clothes for her wear-around-the-house togs, she saw the pink dress. How she'd love to slip it on and go down to dinner in it! Maybe it would give her the morale boost she needed. But that was being silly. Mom and. Dad would be sure to raise their eyebrows and think—what *would* they think? At any rate, it was *not* the thing to wear tonight. Sue patted the dress gently and shut the closet door.

Conversation at the dinner table was strained. Dad could tell she'd been crying, she knew. But no one said anything. Even Kit and Jay didn't mention her reddened nose. After supper was over and the dishes done, Dad called her into the living room. Now she was in for it!

"I understand you were inexcusably rude this afternoon," Dad began.

Sue nodded.

"Any explanation?"

Sue shook her head.

"You mean you have nothing to say—no *reason* to give?" Dad's eyes were probing.

"I just got mad at Mrs. Cannon being such a buttinsky," Sue finally said. "Mom must have told you."

"That's no excuse for bad manners, Sue." Dad sounded stern. "As a member of our family, you are to conduct yourself as a *lady* at all times."

"Yes, Dad." Sue kept her face expressionless.

"Try to understand the woman, Sue. Sometimes if you *know* why people act the way they do, you can excuse them."

"Excuse spying and ratting?" Sue seated herself on the arm of the overstuffed chair and glared at her dad with angry eyes.

"If you are referring to the show episode, Sue, I'd hardly call it 'spying' to witness what went on in the lobby. You were on public display." Dad tamped his pipe and lit it, waiting, apparently, for Sue to go on. When she didn't, he continued carefully, "As for 'ratting,' as you call it, I've heard little or no explanation of that accusation."

Sue remained silent.

"Try to remember, Sue, Mrs. Cannon is a lonely old woman. She has only her house, her garden, and her neighbors to keep her interest. And so she is more than naturally curious about the affairs of others."

"Well, she can just leave me alone." Sue felt her anger boil to the surface again. "I think she's just a sneak."

Dad shook his head. "I'm afraid you've hurt yourself more than her with your outburst." He stopped, then seemed to think his next words out carefully. "Would you like to tell us what happened at school?"

Sue looked at her father. It wouldn't be easy to tell right now—Dad seemed much more sympathetic to Mrs. Cannon than to her. She shook her head.

"All right." Dad looked resigned. "I'm sorry you feel this way. You may go to your room now."

"Thank you." Sue said the words with exaggerated politeness. She walked up the stairs slowly. She closed the door to her room behind her. The door. It was really shut now.

In the days that followed, neither Mom nor Dad mentioned Mrs. Cannon, nor did they inquire much about school. They just seemed to maintain a quiet watchfulness.

Now it was Thursday, violin lesson over with, and just a little time to spare before dinner. Sue sat at the playroom table with Kit and Jay across from her. She squeezed at a lump of clay in her hands.

"Make a bunny, Sue," demanded Kit.

"No, a car," said Jay.

"First a bunny, then a car." Sue laughed as she looked at their eager faces. She handed Kit a piece of blue clay. "Here, Kit, you make the ears." She pushed some red clay to Jay. "You can make the wheels."

Sitting here playing with Jay and Kit, Sue felt happier than she had in days. Maybe it was because they made things so simple. And life these days seemed decidedly complex.

Sue broke the clay into two blobs and placed the smaller on the table. She rolled the bigger piece between her palms until it was smooth and round. If only it were as easy to smooth out her problems as it was the clay. Most of the time, now, it was as though she were two people. The new Sue and the old one. The new Sue was the one who laughed and talked too loudly, the one who linked arms with the girls in The Crowd and walked about the school-yard at noontime. Sometimes they walked four abreast— Sue, Maxine, Judy, and Laura. Other times it was just she and Maxine. Or else they met in the washroom to laugh uproariously at jokes. Or huddled in groups to talk in low whispers about love and life and boys. The new Sue ignored Cathy and Ellen. But they ignored her, too.

She put down the molded body of the bunny and picked up the smaller piece. The old Sue, the one she was being right now, that one was so *comfortable*. If only that one would be at school. Then she would stop laughing at jokes she didn't understand. And she'd tell the girls they were all wrong about love and life and boys. There was that book in her room, *Facts of Life and Love for Teen-agers,* that said they were wrong. And she'd go up to Cathy and Ellen and say, "Hi, I'm sorry I was so stupid. Let's be friends again." If she could only break through Mom and Dad's watchfulness and say. "Hey, there, this is your very own Sue, remember? And I love you." But no, life had turned into a sort of remoteness, a frightening aloofness. Only at moments like this—sitting here with Kit and Jay—did she become wholly herself again.

"Aw, that's no bunny head." Kit grabbed the clay from Sue. "It's still just a round ball."

"Goodness." Sue took the clay back. "I was thinking. I'll do belter." She pushed in the eye spaces and molded the nose. "There," she said, setting the head atop the body. "Now it's ready for the ears."

Kit tried to attach the ears. Jay flattened out the four balls he'd made for wheels. Sue worked quickly at a blob of red clay, forming the car. No matter what, she understood, she was going to get a bid to the Jay Dees. Maxine told her today it had been put in the mail. Maybe then she'd feel as if she really *belonged* somewhere.

"Hey, aren't you finished yet?" Jay shoved at Sue's arm.

"Sure, all done." Sue placed the model on the table.

"Now a duck and a caterpillar," demanded Kit.

"And a plane and a butterfly," added Jay.

"And a cat and a boat and a dog and an elephant, I suppose," finished Sue. She planted a kiss on Kit's nose and ruffed Jay's hair. "But you kids have to do some of the work." She picked up a piece of yellow clay.

"Company, Sue."

"Oh no!" Sue dropped the clay and hid her hands behind her as she saw Mom at the door with Dave. She gave an embarrassed laugh.

"Hi." Dave looked almost as uncomfortable as she felt.

"Sue's making clay things," Jay announced. "Can you make a plane?"

"Oh, Jay," Sue said desperately. "Hush."

Dave gave Sue a half smile. "You think I can't?" he asked. He sauntered over to the table. "To tell the truth, I'm known as the best jet plane modeler in the country." He sat down beside Sue and picked up some clay. "What model, boy?" he asked.

"Any kind," Jay answered. "My name's Jay," he added.

Sue watched Dave work the clay. In a matter of seconds he laid the model before Jay. "Okay?" he asked.

"Yeeeeeeeeooooooooow." Jay put the jet through a power dive.

"You're gooder than Sue," Kit adjudged. "But I love my bunny," she added loyally.

There was no stopping Dave then. He modeled planes, ships, pigs, horses, even the elephant and butterfly. And just when they had the last bit of clay used up and would have to demolish a model or two to make something new, Mom came to the door with what Sue thought was perfect timing.

"Dinner," Mom announced. "We've set a place for you, Dave, if you care to stay."

Sue saw Dave's face color slightly. "Meat loaf and scalloped potatoes," she whispered to him.

"I— well, I——"

"He's nice. He'll stay," Jay stated.

"He's my friend." Kit slipped her hand into Dave's. "He wants to have dinner with me."

"Well, Dave?"

Dave's face was still a dull red. "Yes—that is, if it's no brother."

"The phone's over there." Mom pointed. "And you all better wash the clay off your hands."

Most of the families Sue knew didn't say grace before meals. She wondered if Dave would think them peculiar. It was Jay's turn to give the blessing, and Sue was grateful when she heard Dave's "Amen" join the others.

For a while the meal went awkwardly. There was that moment of silence when a slice of tomato skidded from Dave's plate onto the tablecloth. Sue again had the sensation of perfect timing when Kit chose that moment to knock over her glass of milk. And while Mom mopped up the milk Dave retrieved his tomato almost unnoticed.

After that the tension seemed relieved. Sue admired the way Dad drew Dave out. Jay told about the jet Dave made, and the "men" started talking about planes. Dave, it seemed, loved making models—even had one with an engine. Jay listened so hard he had to be reminded to eat. And Mom flashed Sue a smile that said, "Men! Funny creatures, aren't they?"

Sue and Dave washed and dried the dishes while Mom gave Jay and Kit their baths and got them ready for bed. The two worked together without talking, with just the music from the kitchen radio breaking the silence. It wasn't because they didn't have anything to say. It just seemed better that way.

When the last dish was in the cupboard, Sue led Dave into the living room. Dad was going to read Kit and Jay their good-night stories, and tonight was *The Little Engine That Could*. Sue knew it was childish of her but she never tired of hearing it.

Funny, Sue reflected as Dad's voice rose and fell over the click of Mom's knitting needles, Dave seemed so *gentle* tonight. It was a description she'd never have identified with him before.

"Okay," said Mom as the engine finally steamed down the other side of the mountain. "Time for bed, you two."

"Kiss," demanded Kit as Jay gravely shook hands with Dave.

Dave's arm drew Kit close as he leaned his face over for the kiss. "You're some cutie-pie," Sue heard him whisper.

"My biggest bear hug," Kit announced as she finally released Dave. She bounced around the room, collecting the rest of her good-night kisses and then was off up the stairs.

Dave had such a strange, faraway look on his face that Sue wondered if she should speak. "Do you want to look at TV with Dad—or come into the playroom and hear my new records," she finally said.

"Records." Dave stood up and followed Sue into the playroom.

Sue gestured to her rack. "Take your pick."

Dave handed her a record. She was sure he hadn't even read the label. As the music blared forth, she sat on a chair arm. Dave leaned against the doorway. Now the lack of words seemed uncomfortable.

"That Kit!" Dave spoke finally. "She's some little kid. Reminds me, I guess, of my sister."

"Oh." Sue was surprised. She'd thought Dave was an only child.

"She's dead." Dave's voice was low. "She and Mom—they were killed two years ago in an auto accident. They were going back East to visit my grandmother."

"I'm sorry." Sue knew the words were inadequate, but she couldn't think of a thing else to say.

"Once—once we had a life sort of like yours." Dave's voice cracked, and Sue wondered frantically if he were going to cry. She'd never seen a boy cry. Not a big boy. What would she do?

"I'm sorry," she murmured again.

"Yeah—most people are. Not my dad, though. He gets himself married again." The bitterness in Dave's words was a hurting thing.

"Maybe—well, maybe he just wanted to make a home for you again."

"Oh, sure. That's why he marries some dame just ten years older than me? He doesn't even remember my mother and sister any more. But I do. I always will." Dave reached for his wallet and flipped it open. "Here."

Sue studied the pictures. They both looked so much like Dave. She closed the wallet and handed it back. "I don't think he's forgotten," she said slowly. "He couldn't. It's just that—well, something about life having to go on, I guess."

"Yeah?" The sneer on Dave's face made him almost ugly. "Once it was the four of us together. Now it's two against one. Him and her against me."

Sue turned to the player and flipped over the record. She swallowed hard. What could she possibly say?

"How'd you like it to happen to you?" Dave went on. "How'd you like a stepmother?"

Sue felt her eyes widen as she watched Dave's face. "I can't," she whispered. "I can't even bear to think about it."

Dave's face looked so lost, he looked so defenseless, Sue felt engulfed by the sadness of it. If only the right words would come.

"Sorry." Dave took a deep breath. "I didn't mean to get so sloppy. It's just that Kit reminds me of Sis." He picked up the player arm and started the record again. "Come on, let's dance."

Sue was glad to dance, glad to get away from the hurt look in Dave's eyes. The next record Dave picked was a fast one. They finished in a mad whirl of music. Sue selected a record this time. "My dad's favorite," she said as the lilting notes of. "Stardust" filled the room. They danced slowly this time, hardly moving about the floor. Dave's arm tightened around Sue and his shirt felt cool against her cheek. Then he stopped dancing and dropped his hands to his side. Sue stepped back, wondering.

"Susan." Dave's voice dropped to a whisper in its seriousness. "Susan, will you go steady with me now? Be my girl *really?*"

Sue nodded, unable to speak. She hadn't expected *this*. She remembered that other time—at the Peppermint Prom. But this time he was asking her because he liked her. Not because he was mad at Judy.

Dave unfastened his ID bracelet and put it on Sue's wrist. She held out her arm, looking at the bracelet.

"Looks good, huh?" Dave remarked.

Sue agreed. It looked good. It felt good.

"Let's dance to celebrate." Dave took her hand and pulled her toward him.

"Wait." Sue broke away and dashed into the kitchen. She picked up her purse and unfastened the tiny harmonica. She held it tight in her hand as she walked back into the playroom.

"Well?" Dave looked at her questioningly.

Sue felt a wave of shyness sweep over her. To hand the harmonica to Dave suddenly seemed silly.

"What did you dash off for?" Dave persisted.

"I —" Sue groped for an excuse. "Oh, I just had a stupid idea," she blurted. "I thought maybe you'd like this for your key chain or something." She held the tiny harmonica toward him almost defiantly.

"Say." Dave took the small object and examined it minutely. He took a practice blow. "Say, this is swell." He reached in his pocket, drew out his key chain, and fastened the harmonica to it. "Looks good, huh?"

It did look nice. Sue nodded her agreement.

"This calls for a celebration. Let's get a real hot number." Dave flipped over a few records, selected one, and at the first beat he drew Sue to him and they danced. When the last notes died away, Sue dropped exhausted on the davenport. Dave looked down at her, laughing.

"Cream puff," he teased. "Party pooper."

"Guess I am," Sue admitted.

"No." Sue heard Mom at the door. "I'm the guilty party this time. It's eight-thirty."

"Curfew time for guests," Sue explained. "And I haven't quite finished my homework."

She watched Dave walk down the sidewalk. He paused at the hedge and waved. Was it a kiss he blew to her, she wondered? Back in the living room she stood silent a moment, not knowing quite how to begin.

"Nice fellow," Dad commented. "Not what I expected."

Sue took courage from his words. "Look," she said. "Dave's bracelet. We're going steady. Okay?" She felt as though she were standing tiptoe on the brink of something as she looked from Mom to Dad. What would they say? Would they think it *funny*? Would they say she was "too young"?

"Guess our little girl is growing up," Dad said finally.

"Guess so," echoed Mom.

They were giving their okay! Sue felt a rush of tenderness for her parents surge through her. She gave Dad a big hug. "I love you," she said simply. "I love you both very, very much." She grinned at the tremor in her voice. "I'll finish my homework now," she concluded. At the stairway she stopped and turned toward the living room. "Thank you," she said. "Thank you for being so nice to Dave. He needs it."

It would have been easy to just think about Dave, but Sue resolutely put thoughts of him away as she parsed sentences at her desk. When the last sentence was completed it was time for bed.

The bracelet felt good against her cheek as she snuggled down in the blankets. *Dave. Dave Young.* That was a nice name. It had a nice, clean sound to it.

She relived the evening, step by step. *How'd you like it to happen to you?* Terror gripped her. She slipped out of bed and padded quickly down the hall. She looked down on Jay and Kit so deep in their dreams. She bent over and kissed them gently. If anything ever happened to them . . . if anything ever happened to Mom or Dad . . . Poor Dave. Poor lonely Dave. Sue retraced her steps to her room. Mom always said time healed all things. Dave would need a lot of it. Maybe she and Kit could somehow help. . . . Sue left the door wide open and slipped into bed again. The soft murmur of Mom and Dad talking downstairs was a comforting *warm* sound. . . .

9
The Decision

FOR THE NEXT WEEK, Sue felt as if she were riding on her own private pink cloud. Wearing Dave's ID brought her firmly within The Crowd. And Judy didn't seem to mind—she was going steady with Mo now.

Sue had tried to restore her friendship with Cathy and Ellen. She'd made a point of going up to them, showing them the bracelet. But somehow she sounded as though she was bragging, and Ellen's response was hardly friendly. It was a relief when Maxine dragged Sue away. Ricky and Chester maintained what Mom would have called a bare nodding acquaintance.

At the beginning of the week, Sue had received her official invitation to join the Jay Dees. With it had been instructions for initiation. She'd worn socks that didn't match, her sweater and skirt backwards; she'd done her

hair in two pony tails tied with different-colored ribbons—
and now, today, she wore a jacket with big pockets. She and
Maxine had a "pilgrimage" to make. Just what it was Sue
couldn't imagine. Tonight she'd be initiated. That meant
forgoing the show with Dave, but he seemed pleased that
she was going to be a Jay Dee. In fact, he was going on a trip
with his dad for the weekend.

Sue was glad Maxine had been chosen as her "big sister"
during initiation. Of all the girls in The Crowd, she liked
Maxine best. And tonight's meeting would be at Maxine's.

Dismissal bell rang and Sue ran down the ramp.

"All set?" Maxine's round face beamed.

Sue nodded. "But why all the mystery? Just what is the
'pilgrimage' anyway?"

Maxine gave an excited giggle. "You'll find out when we
get to the Avenue," she promised.

Sue felt her spirits sink. It was bad enough to do whacky
things around school. But on the Avenue! Oh well, other
kids had been initiated, too, and being a Jay Dee would be
worth it. She fell in step with Maxine.

"You know," Maxine confided as they walked along,
"now that you're going to be a Jay Dee, maybe we can be
best friends."

"Why——" Sue groped for the right answer.

"I'm not pretty like the others. And I know I'm not
exciting—or——"

"I'd *like* to be best friends," Sue interrupted firmly. "I like you the best anyway."

Maxine almost wriggled with her delight. "Super," she said. "That's super."

There was something almost pitiful about Maxine's eagerness to "be friends," Sue thought. Maxine didn't seem to have any real friends, she reflected. In The Crowd she was a sort of flunky—the one who ran errands. Was it because she was too appreciative of being allowed in the group?

"Here we are." Maxine stopped in front of the variety store. "And here's your list." She handed Sue a scrap of paper.

Sue read it. *Lipstick, bobby pins, candy bar, ball-point pen.*

"I'll wait here while you get 'em," Maxine said. "They're the things Judy wants."

Sue reread the list. It didn't make sense. Why should she get things for *Judy*? "I don't have any money," she said flatly.

"We know. That's the idea." Maxine's eyes were wide blue pools of excitement. "You have to 'lift' them."

"You mean *steal*? Steal this stuff for Judy?" Sue frowned in her astonishment. The idea of stealing for anyone was—was appalling. It was frightening, too.

"Pooh." Maxine shrugged. "There's nothing the store would miss. You should have seen my list."

"You stole things?"

"It's the final test. It means you'll do *anything* for the Jay Dees."

"The Jay Dees or Judy?"

"Judy takes things, too. She swiped a record for Dave once."

Sue handed the list back to Maxine. "Well, I'm out. Guess I won't be a Jay Dee after all."

"Come on." Maxine tried to press the list back into Sue's hand. "Don't be like this. Please. I want you in the club so badly. It won't hurt anyone. Look, if you feel guilty, why not add up what the loot costs—and put the money in one of those charity jars later or something.".

"No."

"Please. Please, just so we can be best friends?"

"No."

"It's not really wrong. Just a sort of dangerous challenge. It's like winning at a game." Maxine's eyes as well as her voice were pleading now. "For me?"

"Not for you—or for Judy—or to be a Jay Dee. Not for anything." Sue's voice had risen slightly, and Maxine looked around furtively.

"Shhh," cautioned Maxine. "Look over there. Judy's looking. Please—at least come in the store with me for a minute."

Sue followed Maxine's gaze. Judy raised her hand in a salute and Maxine followed suit. Sue didn't even bother to smile. She looked back at Maxine. For some reason Maxine looked almost scared. "Okay, I'll go in the store with you," Sue agreed.

The girls sauntered around the store, looking at this and that. Sue felt positively stupid. She picked up a swatch of hair and tried it on before a mirror. She giggled at her reflection. "You like me as a redhead?" she asked.

Maxine came over and her smile was indulgent. Sue saw the manager eye them and was desperately grateful she wasn't in the store "swiping." His gaze was a most penetrating one. Maxine had moved on to another counter and Sue joined her. "Want to go now?" Maxine said finally.

Sue was glad to get out of the store. Judy was gone. "I'm sorry," she said to Maxine. "Can't we be best friends—even though I'm not a Jay Dee?"

"You will be." Maxine grinned. "All the things are in your pocket."

Sue stopped short. "What? What did you say?"

"You've got 'em all in your pockets. I put them there for you." Maxine looked pleased and proud at her accomplishment.

Sue put her hand into one pocket and then the other. She drew out the lipstick, the bobby pins, the ball-point pen. Yes, even the candy bar was there. She dropped them back as if they burned. She hadn't taken them, but here she was with stolen goods. "Maxine," she wailed. "You—you——"

Maxine laughed. "I didn't mind. We just won't tell Judy how you got them."

"You don't understand. You don't understand at all."
There was shock and wonder in Sue's voice.

"Sure I do." Maxine dragged at Sue's jacket. "Let's get going. You didn't want to swipe things, so I did it for you. We just won't tell Judy. We won't tell anyone."

"That isn't it," Sue exclaimed. "I don't want to have them. I don't want to be a Jay Dee—now."

"There's Mr. Mack," warned Maxine.

Sue looked, scared to the very core of her being. Mr. Mack, who seemed to know everything. Could he know—already—she had stolen goods on her? He couldn't. He was coming in the wrong direction.

"Hello, girls." Mr. Mack's eyes appeared to be smiling at them. Did he notice her bulging pockets, Sue wondered.

"Hello, Mr. Mack." Both girls spoke in unison.

"Been shopping?" he asked.

"Yes—I mean no." Sue felt her face flush under his gaze. Maxine apparently was speechless. "I mean, I have to go home right now." She hurried down the sidewalk, almost dragging Maxine with her.

Maxine broke away from Sue's hold on her arm. "What did you act like that for?" she demanded. "You sure acted funny."

"I feel funny. I want to go home right now." Sue was walking so fast, it was almost a run. Maxine tagged about a step behind. Sue's stomach felt as if it were tied in a knot. There was a dull pain in her side. She wondered for a minute if she were getting sick. The jacket felt as though it were weighed down with rocks. The house had never looked so good as when she and Maxine reached the front steps.

Mom must have seen them coming because she held open the door. "What speed burners," she exclaimed. She greeted Maxine with a smile. "I've a pitcher of lemonade awaiting a couple of thirsty characters."

Maxine flashed a grateful look at Mrs. Stevens, then turned to Sue. "May I—have some lemonade?" she asked.

Sue caught Mom's puzzled expression as she looked from Maxine to Sue. "Of course," Sue said. She followed her mother into the kitchen. Jay and Kit were at the table, lemonade and cookies before them.

"Take off your jacket, Sue," Mother said. "It's so awfully warm."

"No." Sue drew her jacket tight around her. Somehow, if she kept it close, she felt that the things in her pockets wouldn't show.

It seemed to Sue that Maxine sipped her lemonade with maddening slowness. Wouldn't she ever leave? She wondered how Maxine could be so calm and cheerful, chatting with Jay and Kit and answering all Mom's questions gaily. Sue could hardly force herself to drink the lemonade, and her cookie lay untasted.

"Is something wrong, Sue?" Mom turned questioning eyes on Sue.

Sue pretended not to hear.

"Susan," Mom persisted. "What's the matter?"

Sue was almost overwhelmed with the strong desire to tell. Maybe Mom could straighten Maxine out, too, on how wrong it was to—to steal. "I—Mom, today Maxine and I—"

"I've got to be going, Mrs. Stevens." Maxine rose hurriedly, almost upsetting the pitcher of lemonade. "I'll see you tonight, Sue. Okay?"

"She'll be there," Mom agreed.

Sue went to the door with Maxine. "Don't be stupid," Maxine whispered. "Were you going to tell your *mother?*"

Sue didn't answer.

"If you tell her," Maxine continued, "you'll only get her worried—and mad at you. She doesn't *ever* have to know. Besides, she'd never let you be a Jay Dee—or my best friend."

Kit and Jay squeezed by Sue as she stood at the door, wordlessly watching Maxine go her way. Maybe Maxine was right. Mom *would* worry. She'd be terribly upset if Sue told. This was her problem, her very own. One she should work out herself.

With a sudden movement, Sue closed the door and ran up the stairs to her room. She knew now what she had to do. She shook her bank impatiently, trying to dislodge the quarters and dimes she'd put there. Finally she figured she had enough. She dashed down the stairs and out the door.

Kit and Jay were in front of the garage as she went to the side area and got out her bike. It had been a long time since she'd ridden it. Girls at Taft didn't care to be seen riding bikes. As she wheeled it around, she caught Jay's and Kit's look of astonishment. "Tell Mom I'll be right back," she called.

She'd have to hurry, hurry, hurry. The store closed in a few minutes. Sue pedaled with all the energy she had. She took the most direct route, even though it might mean that fellow Taft students might see her. Quickly she parked the bike in the rack on the corner. She quickened her stride down the street. She couldn't stop to think this out—or she'd get scared. But at the store's entrance, Sue's feet seemed leaden. How could she walk in and explain how the things were taken, even though she'd brought the money along to pay for them. She couldn't say Maxine stole them, and *she* certainly hadn't. About the only thing she could do—was return them. And that she'd have to do as cleverly as Maxine had taken them.

Stealthily, Sue went from counter to counter, looking at first this thing, then that. And when she thought a clerk wasn't looking, she slipped an article out of her pocket and put it back in its place. Only the ball pen, now. Then she'd be free. But ball-point pens were up by the cash register. How had Maxine managed to take it? She held the thing in her hand.

"May I help you?"

Sue jumped. The manager was at her elbow.

"I'm just looking—looking at this pen," Sue managed to say.

"How did it get back here with the lipsticks?" the manager asked. "Pens are up by the checking counter. You weren't by any chance trying to walk off with it, were you?"

"No. Oh no."

"Well," the manager hesitated. He was studying Sue's face. "Weren't you in here earlier this afternoon? With another girl—just looking that time too?"

Sue couldn't meet the manager's eyes. Fright made her hands clammy. She stared with a sort of horror at the pen she still had in her hand. Resolutely, she handed the pen to the manager. She swallowed hard to get her words out. "I don't want the pen. I was just looking."

The manager seemed to bristle with suspicion. "We're closing now," he said. "Perhaps it's time for you to leave."

Sue turned blindly to the door. This was almost like the scene in the show. Except not so bad. She almost expected Mrs. Cannon's face to come jeering and leering at her. She should feel clean—and free. She no longer had the things on her. But she still felt horrible. Near the entrance Sue's glance caught the display of bubble soap. She picked up two bottles and handed them hurriedly to the check-out clerk. "I'll take these," she said, trying to be casual.

Now her pockets really bulged. But it was a nice, clean bulge. Sue pedaled back home almost as fast as she'd come. Jay and Kit tagged along as she put her bike away.

"Here's a surprise for you." Sue gave them the two bottles of soap.

Mom was waiting at the door again. "Susan Stevens." Mom looked worried as Sue entered the house. "Where did you go? What in the world are you up to? What is the matter?"

"Nothing, Mom. Not a thing." Sue threw her arms around her mother and planted a kiss on her cheek. "Nothing's wrong—not now."

Mom didn't look quite satisfied with Sue's explanation, but Sue gave her an impish grin and dashed to her room. She felt gay, free—almost lightheaded in her relief. It wouldn't take long, once she got to the meeting, to be on her way home again. Maxine would be hurt—and angry. But that couldn't be helped now.

Tonight Sue would be through with being one of The Crowd. She'd be through being a Jay Dee before she really had become one.

She was through, too, she guessed, with Cathy and Ellen.

Maybe, after tonight, Dave wouldn't have much use for her either. He seemed to think the Jay Dees were something really special.

But as least *she* could stand herself again.

10

Initiation

SUE RAPPED THE KNOCKER sharply on Maxine's door. She was late purposely. She wanted to be sure most of The Crowd was present before announcing her decision. She'd even rehearsed the words she was going to say. This was going to be a clean break, sharp and decisive. She felt good just standing here at the door. The only part she dreaded was facing Maxine. Maxine would be dismayed.

A steady hum of voices and an occasional high-pitched giggle came from inside. Maybe they hadn't heard. She raised her hand to the knocker again as the door was flung open and Maxine drew her eagerly into the house.

"You're late." Maxine sounded reproving. "The meeting's already started. Hurry."

"But, Maxine, I just came to——"

"Come on." Maxine gave another tug and Sue almost

lost her balance. "Madame President, may I present our new *Jay Dee?*"

Sue glanced quickly around the room. There sat Judy, the queen bee, enthroned in a big overstuffed chair. Her face held a gloating, anticipatory look. The other girls were either sitting in chairs or sprawled on the floor, leaning against the furniture. Tonight, it seemed, everyone was present.

Judy banged a gavel against the coffee table. "The meeting will come to order," she announced. "Sue, sit down."

Maxine made room for Sue on the piano bench. Sue remained standing. Now—now was the moment to tell. "Madame President," she began.

"Quiet," Judy commanded. "Get to work, girls."

Sue felt rather than saw Maxine slip the blindfold over her eyes. Two girls had pinned her arms to her side.

"Now," Sue heard Judy say, "you're to co-operate, Sue, and you won't get hurt. Otherwise——"

Sue was guided to a bench and told to sit down. She hadn't counted on this. Before she could have her say, the initiation was started. Well, let them have their fun. And then she'd tell them.

"Sue," Maxine said quietly, "put out your hands. Tell us what you feel."

Sue felt her hand being shoved into a bowl. The things she touched were cold and slimy. She almost laughed. How corny. Wet macaroni or spaghetti, that's what it was. Why, she'd seen this trick years ago at a Halloween party.

"What do you feel?" Maxine repeated.

Sue gave a delicate shudder. "Worms," she said. "Wiggly, slimy worms." She heard the peals of laughter from the girls.

"Eat one, Sue. Eat one."

Sue took the one placed in her hand and raised it gingerly to her mouth. It tasted like nothing. Well-almost nothing. What if it *wasn't* macaroni? She almost gagged at the thought and returned the uneaten portion to the dish.

"Now this, Sue. Try this."

Her hand was plunged into another bowl. This time she felt things that were round and cold and slippery. Peeled grapes, she decided.

"Fish eyes," the girls declared. "Eat, Sue, eat."

The grape taste was real, and Sue sighed her relief.

"One more thing. Stand up." She felt a hand guide her. "Now step."

Sue stepped. She was on a board now. She knew this trick, too. But the girls were going to extremes. She felt she'd surely lose her balance as the board was raised up—up—up.

"Jump." This was Judy's voice.

Sue jumped. The floor was surprisingly close, and she almost lost her balance.

She pulled off her blindfold. The girls were almost doubled up with laughter. She joined in. She'd been right about the grapes and the macaroni. And then her stomach did a flip-flop. There, on top of the macaroni was—*half* a worm. Sue swallowed hard as her stomach churned wildly. What if it weren't a ruse—what if she'd—— She searched the faces around her. Maxine. Had she actually *winked* at her? Judy's face was flushed with excitement, and her eyes were almost feverishly bright.

"The forfeit, Sue. Now the forfeit," demanded Judy. "Then you can sign the book."

Sue fought with the nausea that threatened her as she again caught sight of the macaroni dish. She swallowed. "What forfeit?" she managed to ask.

"Why, the things you—ah—*got*—on the Avenue."

This was it. Now . . . now . . . "I took them back," she announced, her voice loud and clear.

"You *what?*" Judy was on her feet, her eyes narrow slits as she looked at Sue. "No one can be a Jay Dee without fulfilling *all* the requirements."

"That's why I took them back. I don't want to be a Jay Dee."

Sue heard Maxine gasp. She turned and looked at the girl. Her round cheeks were white, and her lips quivered as though she was going to cry.

"I'm sorry, Maxine, but I couldn't do it. I took 'em back

after you left." She faced Judy again. "I won't steal—or be a part of stealing—for you, or anyone, or anything," she announced flatly.

"So." Judy walked up to Sue until her face was just inches away. How could she look so just right and poised when her eyes blazed with hate and fury? Sue backed away.

"So," Judy repeated. "You go through our initiation—through all our plans—and just quit?"

"Yes."

"No." Judy almost spat the word. Now her mouth that Sue thought was so lovely was a sneering, scornful slit.

"Skip it, Judy." Laura spoke up now. "Let her go. Drop her. She's not worth the bother."

"No." Judy looked around the room, her eyes seeming to take in everyone. "And I'll tell you why. She knows too much. And she's just the type who would squeal."

"No, I won't really," Sue protested. "I'll pretend I don't even know you."

"Furthermore," Judy went on, ignoring Sue, "she'll be a *good* Jay Dee—or else."

"Or else—what?" Sue heard her voice crack. She was suddenly afraid. But why?

Judy shrugged. "We might let it be known on the Avenue that you—ah—*take* things?"

"I don't."

"And they'll believe us—because we'll have proof."

Judy's smile was a taunt. "And if that's not enough, maybe something will happen to someone. Not you, but someone you like."

"You wouldn't dare." Sue almost whispered the words.

"I wouldn't?" Judy was laughing at her openly now. "Maybe not. But then again, maybe I would. Could you take a chance?" Judy's giggle was almost hysterical, and the look in her eyes was a wild, cruel thing. "Ask Chester what happened to his Sunday suit one night, why don't you?

"You wouldn't dare," Sue repeated, but her words didn't convince even her. Judy *would* dare. Judy would dare anything. Sue's glance went again to the dish of macaroni. Judy was the one who thought of the worm—who would slice it in two. Fear and apprehension swept over her as Sue sank weakly onto the arm of a chair.

"Secretary," Judy said triumphantly, "get the book. She can sign in blood."

Slowly, as though she were in a dream, Sue pricked her finger with the needle Maxine handed her and squeezed it until a drop of blood showed. With a shaky hand, she signed her name in the notebook Laura put before her. She brushed her hand across her face and looked around at the girls as she straightened up. They were all so quiet, so absolutely still. Were they afraid—too?

"Okay." Judy banged the gavel on the coffee table again, once more the poised, sure queen bee. "Meeting adjourned. Let's listen to records, Maxine."

Sue felt as if she were in a trance as Maxine turned on the hi-fi. She sank down onto an ottoman as the first loud notes of a downbeat record filled the room. The girls were talking now, enthusiastic, gay, laughing. Judy seemed to be the brightest of them all. Sue watched, miserably alone. Maxine inched her way over.

"Don't be like that," Maxine whispered. "Everything is all right. Really. Now you're a Jay Dee everything's fine. It's just that Judy doesn't like to be crossed."

Sue couldn't find the words to answer.

"Look," Maxine went on, "Judy's just kidding. She wouldn't *do* anything—not really. And now we can be best friends."

Sue half smiled and squeezed Maxine's hand. Maybe Maxine didn't believe Judy, but *she* did. She could tell by the look in Judy's brown eyes. She saw Judy come over toward her.

"Having fun?" Judy's question was an open sneer.

"Naturally." Sue made her words drip sarcasm. "This is simply tops." She made her eyes meet Judy's bright gloating glance defiantly, unafraid.

"Hey," called Laura, "when do we eat?"

"Right now." Maxine scuttled out of the room and came back in a moment, followed by her parents.

Sue looked at the trays of hot chocolate and doughnuts with acute distaste. She didn't see how she could force a bite past her lips.

"Mom, Dad," said Maxine, "you've never met our newest member, have you? This is Sue Stevens."

"Glad to meet you, Sue." Mrs. Henning placed the tray on a table and proffered her hand.

Sue felt her fingers clammy in Mrs. Henning's warm clasp.

"A new member? This calls for a picture," said Mr. Henning. He left the room as the girls grabbed for the doughnuts. In a moment he was back, and Sue was posed between Judy and Laura while the flash bulbs went off.

How can you be so dumb! Sue thought as she watched the Hennings mix with the girls. *How can you not know what kind of a club this is?* And yet, she hadn't known—until today—had she?

It seemed like centuries before Dad came to pick her up, yet when she looked at the clock it was only eight-thirty. As she bid her good-bys, Dad asked if anyone would like a ride, maybe.

"Oh, Mr. Stevens, if it really wouldn't be too much bother——" cooed Judy, and Sue found herself followed to the car by both Judy and Laura.

Sue sat silently in a corner as the girls chatted with Dad. And then they were finally at Judy's.

Judy jumped out of the car. "Thanks so much, Mr. Stevens," she said. She turned to Sue. "Gee, your dad's a honey," she went on. And then she looked hard at Sue.

"Good-by, new Jay Dee," she said in a low voice. "Remember." And she ran her finger across her throat.

Dad caught the gesture. He laughed as he drove off. "Is that one of your good-night signals?" he asked. "I can remember having a secret lodge grip."

"I—I guess it is," Sue murmured.

"It's a goody," said Laura. "Just like our club is."

When they reached her home, Laura repeated Judy's farewells as though she were a ditto machine. Sue saw Dad beam at the compliment. Then Laura turned to Sue. "Remember, Jay Dee," she said. And she, too, ran her finger across her throat.

"Beats me," Dad said as they drove off. "When I was a kid, that wasn't a particularly *friendly* gesture."

It isn't now, either, Sue wanted to confess. But Judy and Laura had sealed her lips.

Mom greeted them at the door. "Well, honey, have fun?" she asked, and then went on without waiting for Sue's answer. "I guess we were wrong, Dad, about Sue not belonging."

"They're nice kids," Dad said. "Especially that Judy. She's a real charmer."

Mom smiled. "Well, if it's what Sue wants——"Her voice trailed off. "But I do wish you would still be friends with Cathy and Ellen. I'm so fond of them." She patted. Sue on the arm. "I must confess I miss those two."

I do too, Sue thought, *oh I do, too. So very, very much.* But tonight she had severed the ties. Irrevocably. There was no going back. She was alone—so very much alone. If only she could tell Mom and Dad. But no. If she did, they'd make her drop Jay Dees—and then—well, Judy's threat was still there, a big, gigantic thing.

"Cocoa, Jay Dee?" Mom asked.

Sue shook her head. "We had refreshments at Maxine's." She yawned elaborately. "I'm tired. I think I'll go to bed."

11

Nightmare

"NO, NO, DON'T," SUE screamed. "Don't." But the monster came nearer with a chortling, evil laugh. Its eyes blazed cruelly. She clutched the crumbling rock frantically, but the monster leered at her and pried her fingers loose. And then she was hurtling, down—down—down—with the monster's high, shrill, girl laugh following her. "No," she screamed again as she swirled into black nothingness and knew she was going to hit bottom. At that instant she jerked awake and lay shaking in her bed, her breath coming rapidly, the sobs still inside her.

Another nightmare! She'd had them all night long. Last time she awoke it was still dark. Now her clock said six. This was Saturday, and it would be at least two hours before anyone else in the house stirred. She didn't want to go back to sleep. She drew a long, shuddering breath and sat up. She shook her head, trying to clear away the last vestige of the dream—of the monster with Judy's laugh and eyes.

Should she read—or turn on the radio? No. She might fall asleep again. Sue swung her legs over the side of the bed and walked softly to the window. The sun was casting a few rays across the lawn, and the dew on the grass sparkled like silver and gold beads. She'd mow the lawn, that's what she'd do. She slipped into her old pedal pushers and sneakers. She pulled a sweater over her head. As she started to close the closet door, her pink dress caught her eyes. Lovely, lovely pink dress—a sort of early morning cloud pink. She'd had a lovely, lovely time the evening she'd worn it, too. Dave. She let herself feel the smooth, clean pinkness of it. Could you really feel pink? And then she resolutely closed the door. Quietly she let herself out into the garage and rolled the lawn mower across the driveway.

The grass was so wet, Sue slipped off her sneakers. The dew was shivery cold against her bare feet. It felt good. No nightmares here in a new morning. Here was the energetic reality of pushing the mower across the lawn. But there was also the reality of last night's meeting. She was a Jay Dee—and she was afraid.

As she worked on, Sue began to wonder if maybe she'd just imagined Judy's eyes were cold and relentless, or blazing with cruelty. Nothing would really happen. Judy just liked to talk big. Lots of people were like that. Bragging, boasting, threatening—and doing nothing. Wasn't there something about a bark being worse than a bite? Besides, you couldn't prove something that wasn't—or could you? Sue hadn't taken anything from the store *but would the manager believe it?* She shivered. She could almost hear Judy. *Maybe something will happen to someone—someone you like.*

Sue gave a violent push at the lawn mower. *Ask Chester what happened to his Sunday suit one night.* All right, she would. She'd do just that. She'd ask Chester. She'd call Judy's bluff. But why—why did she have this funny feeling that maybe Dave was involved? Judy hadn't said so. Hadn't even hinted. Was it just because he was a member of the male half of The Crowd? Or was it because Ricky and Chester evaded her these days?

Oh well, pretty soon she'd know. Chester would tell her. Sue sighed with relief. Now she'd decided. Now she had a plan of action. She tackled the lawn again with fresh vigor. It was always better to *know* than to guess.

She had almost finished clipping the edges before Sue heard signs of life from the house. She heard the window in her parents' room go up. As she looked up, Dad waved a greeting. "Hey, early bird," he said, "what are you after— worms? Come on in for breakfast."

Worms. She shuddered, remembering initiation, but she laid aside the edgers, picked up her sneakers, and went around to the kitchen door.

"Mom," Sue said as she attacked her second waffle. "I want to call Chester after breakfast."

"Why certainly, dear."

"Well, I thought maybe that business of not calling boys——"

"If it's a business call——"

"It is, sort of."

"Then of course you may, dear, *after* you've done your chores."

Sue worked through her jobs stolidly, glad to be doing something, yet anxious to *know*. At last she was ready. She dialed the number swiftly. She listened to the rings—one—two—three—four—they just couldn't be out. And then she heard Mrs. Duval's prim "Hello."

"Chester? Oh, my dear, I'm sorry," Mrs. Duval purred sweetly into Sue's ear. "He's at the library. I'll tell him you called. He'll be so disappointed."

Not half as much as I am thought Sue as she hung up the receiver. Now there was nothing to do but wait—or go to the library. And she couldn't stand to wait.

Chester was alone at the table with books stacked in three piles before him when Sue slipped into a chair beside him. "Hi, Chester," she greeted.

Chester looked up, startled. "Why—hi."

"Working on something?" Sue knew her question was inane when obviously he was doing just that.

"Yes. Our science report. I'm looking up planets. Is that why you're here—to work on yours?"

"No." Sue drew a doodle on the table with her finger. "I came up just to see you."

"Me?" Chester's eyes squinted as he looked at her, puzzled. "Why?"

"I—well, this is a sort of silly thing, but someone said something about your Sunday suit." Sue kept her gaze on her fingers as she spoke.

"Sunday suit?" Chester sounded scared, and Sue glanced at him quickly. "You heard about my Sunday suit?"

"Not—well, not exactly. I was just told to ask about it."

"By who?" Chester's eyes had a wary, evasive look about them.

"Whom," Sue corrected automatically. "By Judy," she went on. "She mentioned it last night. Was there something?"

Chester seemed to swallow with an effort. He forgot to keep his voice at a whisper. "Go away," he demanded. "Go away and leave me alone. You're Dave's girl. You belong to The Crowd. Forget you know me. Now scram." He reached for a book and started leafing furiously through the pages, but his glance kept darting around the room.

"There was something about your Sunday suit." Sue spoke slowly, measuring her words. "I guess maybe it had something to do with Judy. I can't see what there is about a suit to *scare* anybody, though."

"Go away." Chester sounded frantic now.

"Did Dave have anything to do with a Sunday suit? Your suit?"

"Go away," Chester repeated. Sue felt a hand on her shoulder. She looked up. The librarian stood there.

"What's the trouble, you two? Don't you believe in signs? Any more noise, and you'll have to leave."

"It's my fault." She pushed back her chair and stood up. "I'll leave." As she pushed open the door, Sue shot a final glance at Chester. He huddled over the table as though he were trying to be as small and inconspicuous as possible. *Now what?*

Sue felt a slump in her own back as she walked down the sidewalk. All this way and she'd found out—nothing! But no, that wasn't quite accurate. She'd found out there was something about Chester's Sunday suit. But what? This was positively silly, getting worked up about a suit. It was silly, too, to have it emerge as a sort of sinister mystery.

The suit involved Judy—and The Crowd. Dave, too, probably. Funny she'd heard nothing about it. Chester was usually a blabber mouth. Had it—whatever "it" was—happened lately? Or a long time ago? Before she'd started going with Dave, that was for sure.

Ricky would know. Even though Chester hadn't mentioned anything to Sue or Cathy or Ellen, he'd have told Ricky. Sue retraced her steps past the library and turned down Ricky's street. Rick had never failed her yet.

Ricky had the hose going full force against the car as Sue approached his house. He turned the water onto the sidewalk, dangerously close to her feet. "What's doing, Sue?" he asked, with his perpetual broad grin lighting his face.

Sue felt her spirits rise. This was like old times—being around a teasing, fun-loving Ricky. "Bet I beat you on ambition," she answered. "I've already mowed our lawn."

Ricky reached over and turned off the water. "And now you're going to help me wash the car. We missed you at the show last night."

"Cathy and Ellen went?" It was more of a question than a statement.

Rick nodded. "Going to help with the car, Sue?"

She made a face at him. "I'm not that ambitious. I'm just out for information."

"You came to the right source. Know-it-all Rick. That's me." Rick's grin gave Sue a confident, warm feeling. "Ask on."

Suddenly Sue didn't want to ask on. She wanted things to be just as they were. She wanted Ricky to stay the same kidding, jolly boy. If she asked, it would mean—what? This was like diving off a big high board into a pool, and she hated diving. She took a deep breath. "It's about Chester," she said. "I want to know about his Sunday suit."

"Sunday suit?" Ricky's grin faded, but his tone was still light. "Now what ever made you ask about a suit, of all things?"

"Not 'a suit,' Ricky, Chester's Sunday suit. Don't evade," Sue pleaded. "Something happened about Chester's Sunday suit. And I want to know what."

"Aren't Chester's clothes his business?"

I guess so.

"Then ask him. It's his business. Not mine."

"I did, Ricky, and—and he just looks scared."

"Well, now I'm looking scared."

"Ricky!" Sue felt like stamping her foot. "Stop evading me. I want to know. I've got to know. It has something to do with The Crowd. I want to know what."

"I'll tell you just one thing, Susan Stevens." Ricky's voice was grim. "Stay away from The Crowd."

"I'm a Jay Dee, Ricky. I can't."

Ricky looked at her as though he had difficulty letting the words sink in.

"Stevens," he said finally. "I didn't believe you could be so dumb." He paused a moment. "The only thing for you to do now is resign."

"I can't, Rick."

"That's stupid to say. You can if you want to. You're your own boss."

Didn't she wish she was! If only she could explain to Ricky. "I can't," she repeated.

Ricky took a deep breath. "I hate to say this, Sue," he said, his gaze a somber, steady thing. "If you're a Jay Dee

then stay away from me. I just don't want to get mixed up—
or messed up." His gaze dropped. "All my life I've wanted
to be a doctor. I'm not taking any chances."

His words were like a slap across the face. "You're the
one who's being stupid," Sue blazed at him. "Stupid and
dumb." She felt her face flush and her eyes fill with tears.
"You—you——" she started, then she spun on her heel and
raced down the street.

Ellen . . . Cathy . . . Chester . . . and now Ricky. They
were all against her. Just because she was a Jay Dee. Just
because she'd been accepted—and they hadn't. Jealous,
that's what they were. She'd show them. She'd be the best
Jay Dee ever. But Chester and Ricky—they weren't really
jealous. They were scared. Of what? Were they afraid—just
as she'd been last night? Chester's Sunday suit! What was
the mystery? Only one person to ask now—Dave. The boys
in The Crowd—had they threatened Chester—and maybe
Ricky—as Judy had threatened her? Was Dave involved?
Mo, now, she could see Mo doing mean things. She *knew*
he did them. And she knew how, when his parents had
been summoned to school about them, they'd just said
"boys will be boys." But Dave—not Dave. Not the Dave
who made clay planes for Jay and pigs for Kit. *The Dave
who hated his dad and stepmother?*

As Sue approached her own block, she saw Mrs. Cannon working in the yard again.

"Hello, there, Sue." Mrs. Cannon sounded as friendly as though there'd been no trouble between them.

"Hi." Sue kept her voice merely polite.

"Some friends were by looking for you." Mrs. Cannon's squinty eyes sparkled. "Your new friends—Judy and Laura they said their names were."

"Oh?"

"I told them you were probably with that handsome Dave—or your old pal, Ricky."

Sue managed a weak smile. "Thanks, Mrs. Cannon," she said. She hurried on. Judy and Laura. Why had they come by? Were they checking up on her? Why was she so— so scared? Was this the way Ricky felt about The Crowd?

12

Dinner Date

WAITING AND WORRYING WERE no fun at all. Sue thought Monday would never come. On Monday she could ask Dave. Mom had shed no light on the reason for Judy's and Laura's visit, and they neither returned nor did they phone. Even Maxine didn't call. Maybe she was embarrassed over the meeting. If only Dave were home. It seemed almost too much that this weekend should be the one on which Dave's dad decided to take him along on his sales trip.

"Just wanted to get me out of Alison's hair, I guess," Dave had said when he told Sue of the trip.

Sue looked puzzled.

"My stepmother," Dave explained.

"Why can't you think he wants you along because you're *you*?" Sue asked. Dave's negative attitude toward his dad bothered her.

Dave shrugged. "I'd rather stay home so I could see you. Now—now Sue wished he had.

By Monday morning Sue felt ready to burst. She gathered up her books and violin and started off to school. She'd see Dave at lunch time. But she'd reckoned without the Jay Dees. At lunch time they enveloped her. Maxine insisted she join the gang and talk. And Dave seemed to be equally enveloped by the male gang. Was it deliberate, this keeping Dave and her apart? Maybe she wouldn't even see him after school.

When classes were over and Sue had retrieved her violin from the music room, she was almost afraid to look to see if Dave were waiting. But there he was, leaning against the street sign.

"Sue Stevens," he said, and his face broke into a delighted grin. "I missed you." He took her violin case from her hand. "But I sure had fun," he added. "It was just like old times." He reached for her hand. "I'll tell you all about it."

For the first time since she'd known him, Sue found herself outtalked. Dave went into minute descriptions of every place he'd seen, every meal he'd eaten. Sue was reduced to mere exclamations of surprise or delight. Dave talked on and on. There was no stopping at the creamery. He talked her right up to the front door; right into the kitchen, as a matter of fact, where he launched into a fresh description of his trip—this time for Mom.

Sue sat and watched, enjoying every minute. This was such a gay, happy Dave. A Dave she'd never really met before. All too soon it was time for Dave to go home. It wasn't until she'd shut the door behind him that Sue remembered she hadn't even mentioned initiation—or Chester's Sunday suit. When he phoned that evening, she still didn't mention it. Asking him face to face would be so much better. By Tuesday evening Sue faced up to the fact that *she didn't want to know.* Dave, as he was right *now,* was just right. And it couldn't make any difference—not really—what had gone before.

The days that followed were so calm and serene that Sue sometimes wondered if maybe she hadn't imagined the initiation—and Judy's threat. If only Cathy and Ellen and Chester and Ricky could be friends with her. But there was a security in belonging to The Crowd. The girls were fun, too, even though she never felt close to them. Maxine was a devoted best friend. Even more so than Ellen or Cathy had been. She was so willing to fall in with any of Sue's suggestions that she wondered if Maxine *did* have a mind of her own. Judy—Sue knew she'd never be friends with Judy. She didn't want to. But they had a sort of truce, she and Judy.

Life fell into pretty much of a pattern. Dave walked her home from school every day. Sometimes they stopped at the creamery. Dave would stay for dinner at Sue's house at least once a week. And Jay and Kit were just wild about him. Mom and Dad seemed to like him, too, and sometimes Sue would wonder when this dreamy, perfect time would end—when Dave would say he liked another girl.

And then one night Dave asked Sue to have dinner at his home. "I know you probably don't want to. It's really all Alison's fault. She says I can't go on mooching meals off your folks unless you have dinner at our house sometimes." The old bitterness had crept into Dave's voice. "Dad agrees."

"Tomorrow," Dave said when he asked Mom. "If it's all right with you."

"Of course, Dave."

"We want to go too," Jay announced.

"Not this time." Mom gave Jay a swat on his jeans. "This is strictly Sue's party."

"It's not a party, Mrs. Stevens." Dave sounded shocked.

"A figure of speech." Mom smiled at Dave. "And don't worry. Sue won't disgrace you."

Sue gave Mom an annoyed look. Every once in a while Mom went too far with her humor.

By the time Dave came to pick her up the next evening, Sue wondered if Mom had meant to be funny, or if she'd been seriously trying to give Sue—and Dave—self-confidence. Even trying to decide what to wear had sent Sue into a tizzy. The pink dress seemed just the thing—until she remembered Dave's shocked face at the idea of a party. She finally decided on a blouse and skirt. If only she could do and say the right things. This dinner meant so much to Dave.

Sue applied her Pink Perfection lipstick carefully. She eyed her reflection with disgust. If only the warm spring sunshine didn't give her so many freckles. She looked like a—like a speckled trout. And who could be proud of bringing a speckled trout home for dinner—unless it was to eat? Poor Dave, stuck with bringing a *fish* to dinner.

"Be back early," Mom reminded them as she opened the front door.

"Eight o'clock," Dave promised. And then they were walking—toward Dave's.

"What—what's she like? Alison, I mean." Sue tried desperately for the familiar feeling of ease.

"Well—uh—I guess she's sort of pretty." Dave seemed floundering for words. "Of course, she's pretty fat."

"Your dad, what's he like—really?"

"What do you mean 'really'? He's just a guy with two arms and legs, a head with a mouth and two eyes and . . . Sorry, Sue." Dave's eyes were unhappy as he looked down on her. He seemed to be getting unhappier with every step. He resented this dinner date. And Sue could feel apprehension mount within her. Dave—as he'd been lately—was lots of fun. But she could still recall that he'd been downright rude on occasions. Was this the way he'd be tonight?

By the time they reached Dave's house, Sue was ready to break away and run back to the security of home with Mom and Dad. She stood at the front door, nervously smoothing down her skirt. Dave opened the door. "We're here," he called. He ushered Sue into the hall.

The kitchen door swung open, and Sue saw a young woman hurry to meet them.

"Alison, this is Sue," Dave introduced. "Sue, this is my stepmother."

"Hello, Mrs. Young." Sue tried hard for a relaxed smile as she proffered her hand.

"I'm glad you could come, Sue." Sue could feel Mrs. Young's hand tremble as she took hers. Why—why, she was scared. Mrs. Young was even more nervous than Sue and Dave were. She turned to Dave. "Your dad phoned. He's sorry that he had to be a few minutes late."

"He would," Dave muttered under his breath.

Sue looked quickly at Mrs. Young, wondering if she'd heard. Her face was flushed and Sue knew she had.

"Would you like to wait in the living room—or watch TV in the den?" Mrs. Young asked.

"Can't I help—in the kitchen? Mom says I'm pretty good—sometimes." As soon as she'd said the words Sue wished she could recall them. Maybe Mrs. Young was one of those people who hated to have guests in the kitchen.

"Why——" Mrs. Young hesitated only the briefest

moment. "Surely you may, Sue," she said, and flashed a welcoming smile. "Maybe Dave would like to help too."

"Not me." Dave settled himself on the kitchen stool and folded his arms, while Sue busied herself with the salad. Dave hadn't been kidding when he said his stepmother was pretty. She was practically beautiful. And as for being fat . . . well, she was wearing a smock, and it probably wouldn't be too long before Dave had a brother or sister. Half brother or sister, Sue corrected herself. Could that be another reason Dave was so resentful?

The small talk was very small, Sue decided as she arranged slices of avocado and oranges on the lettuce leaves. And Dave wasn't helping at all as he sat glowering on the stool. It was with relief she heard the front door open, and Dave's dad walked into the kitchen. He gave his wife a hearty kiss before he turned for introductions. Sue was shocked at the look of pain and aversion on Dave's face as he shifted his gaze from them to her.

The four of them were soon seated at the dinner table. Alison had worked hard to make the dinner a perfect one. Tiny biscuits with the salad. A table set to perfection. If only they could all relax. Sue found herself answering questions in sentences of no more than three words. When Mrs. Young got up to remove the salad plates, Sue jumped up, eager to help, to get away from Mr. Young's gaze just a minute or two. As she did, her arm knocked against her glass of milk, and to her horror she saw it spill across the biscuits and over the tablecloth.

"Oh no." Sue stood aghast as the milk spread in an ever-widening circle. She turned her stricken gaze on Dave. "I'm sorry," she said. If only Dave would forgive her this mess.

His face was scarlet. "Remember," he said, and he choked, and Sue realized he was struggling against laughter. "Remember," he continued, "how I goofed with the tomato—and Kit spilled her milk?" And then the laughter he'd struggled to control came out in big gasps.

Sue could feel the corners of her mouth twitch as she felt the giggles swell up in her throat. She mopped at the spilt milk, feverously trying to control her giggles.

"My goodness, Sue, it's nothing," Mrs. Young said as she mopped along with Sue. "Once I spilled tea down a teacher's back."

With that Sue burst into laughter, and soon the four of them were laughing in almost a chorus. And as if by magic—milk magic—the air was cleared.

The rest of the evening raced by, and Sue was surprised and sorry when Dave said "Gee, it's eight already. And I promised your mother, Sue."

"It's been fun getting to know you, Sue," Mr. Young said as he clasped her hand warmly in his. "You're the first friend Dave's brought home since—since we moved here."

Mrs. Young's smile was tremulous as she added her

good-bys, and Sue was somehow reminded of Kit. She leaned over impulsively and kissed Mrs. Young on the cheek. "Thanks," she said. "Thanks for a lovely evening." And then she was hurrying down the stairs, her hand in Dave's.

"I like them," she told Dave. "They're fun."

"Yeah. Dad's a nice guy."

"I like her, too," Sue insisted. "She's darling."

"She's just showing off." Dave's voice had a belligerent note in it. "She makes it look as if we're friends." His face was set in stubborn lines. "But I've got her number. And I let her know every day that my mom still isn't forgotten."

"Oh, Dave."

"You think I'm silly?"

"No. Cruel. How could she forget?"

"She's having a baby—to make Dad forget."

"No. I don't think so." Sue thought her words out carefully. "She's having it for a—a sort of fresh start. And I'm glad."

"First my dad—and now you." Dave sounded bitter.

"Look, Dave." Sue groped for the right things to say. "I didn't know your mother. But I know she was wonderful—because she had you. But Alison is trying. Not to be your mother. But to be your friend. I can tell."

"Okay, okay, let's forget it. Maybe you're right." Dave's voice suddenly softened. "What I want to ask you—will your parents let you go to the Jay Dee party Judy's giving? It's a date party, you know."

Sue felt herself suddenly tense. The Jay Dee party. It could be fun—just as the Jay Dees had been fun. Mom and Dad would say yes, Sue was sure, providing the party was properly chaperoned. But at Judy's house! She really didn't have much choice about the party actually. It was a Jay Dee doing, wasn't it? If only it weren't at Judy's. Judy—the initiation—and Chester's suit came strongly to mind. Now—now was the time to ask.

"Dave," she said. "Promise you'll tell me something I want to know."

"I promise." Dave looked as though he were laughing at her.

"What happened to Chester's Sunday suit?"

"What?"

"What happened to Chester's suit?"

Sue felt Dave's hand stiffen as he held hers. "What do you mean, what happened to his suit?"

"Just that."

"Why not ask him?"

"I did—and I asked Ricky. It has something to do with Judy and no one tells me anything."

"I won't either. Except to say all that's past. And it wasn't too bad."

"You promised."

"Look, Sue. I can't break a promise to keep a promise. So forget it." Dave's voice was hard.

"But, Dave."

"Forget it, Sue." His voice broke slightly. "Only remember this. I'll never let anything—not anything—ever happen to hurt *you*." And he held her hand as if he would never let it go.

That night, as Sue tried vainly to fall asleep, the three boys and their voices seemed to circle around and around in her mind.

"Go away" said Chester, and his eyes were fear-filled.

"Stay away" Ricky repeated.

"Forget it" said Dave.

So—it was something over and past. Maybe she should forget it. But anxiety didn't go away when you told it to. It stayed, like—like the gnawing pain in her side. It got dull, sometimes. And for long times she'd forget it. And then it would be a sharp, stabbing thing. Maybe she should mention to Mom about the pain sometimes. If only she could tell Dad about the worry.

13

First Kiss

THE DAY STARTED IN a perfectly ordinary fashion, this day of Judy's party. Classes, study, the same dull routine. By the end of the lunch hour, however, Sue could feel the excitement well in her.

"It's going to be super," Judy announced. "The best, the most different party ever."

Sue and Maxine were sitting a little apart from the rest of the Jay Dees, who were standing in a group, talking.

"Have you ever been to Judy's parties?" Sue asked.

"Uh huh! They're really good." Maxine's round face beamed. "Last time we played kissing games."

"Oh."

"Haven't you ever played kissing games?"

Sue shook her head. It would be downright embarrassing to admit she hadn't even been to a boy-girl party since

Ricky's mother had taken them to the beach way back in fifth grade.

"I even got to kiss Dave," Maxine announced triumphantly.

Sue tried hard not to let resentment show on her face. She didn't like the idea of Dave kissing girls. Why, he'd never even tried to kiss her. Not that she'd let him, but at least he could have *tried*. She wondered what it would be like—kissing Dave.

"Judy says that stuff is childish," Maxine said. "Kissing games are out. She's planned something even better."

Sue turned her head to hear what Judy was saying. "We'll have the rumpus room to ourselves," Judy declared. She turned to Sue. "You're coming for sure?"

Sue nodded. "Dave's picking me up."

"Good." Judy gave Maxine a broad wink. "It wouldn't be a party—without Sue, would it?" She patted Sue patronizingly on the shoulder, laughed, and turned back to the other girls.

As Sue sat in class that afternoon she had a hard time concentrating on her studies. That laugh of Judy's! Was it friendly—or ridiculing? Was Sue going to be the butt of a joke. "*I wont let anyone hurt you*" Dave had promised. Did humiliation come under the heading of hurt?

Sue felt as though her stomach was tied in a knot. She tried to relax. She shouldn't get so worried. After all, Judy's parents would be around. She rested her face against her palm. Her hands were icy—or was it just that her face was so hot. The knot in her stomach was an ache that felt better when she bent way over her desk. If she told Mom and Dad how odd she felt they wouldn't let her go. And she'd promised Dave. If only Dave wouldn't be disappointed in her at the party.

Sue was glad Dave just walked her to the front door after school.

"I'm tired," she told Mom. "May I take a nap?"

Mom's surprised look almost made Sue giggle, except that nothing seemed very funny. "A good idea," Mom agreed.

Sue set her hair in pin curls, then crawled into bed. It felt good: warm and secure, and she was being positively stupid, feeling this way before a party.

She woke up just before dinner, feeling a little better. She ate her food determinedly, hoping it would quell the queasy feeling she had.

"Susie's pink," Jay announced as she ate her ice cream.

Mom looked at her sharply. "You are flushed, dear. Feel okay?"

Dad placed his hand on Sue's forehead. "A little warm, maybe," he said. "Excited over the party, I guess."

Sue was glad to get away from the table to take her shower and get ready. Mom had the pink dress neatly pressed and hanging from the light bracket. After her shower, Sue patted herself liberally with Mom's favorite bath powder. She wrapped her robe around her and hurried back to her room. Jay and Kit were sitting cross-legged on her bed.

"We came to see you get pretty," Kit said.

"And Mom says to hurry," Jay finished.

Sue hurried into her underwear. She bent over to put on her shoes.

"Pink Sue," said Jay. "Pink-pink Sue."

She straightened up suddenly to look in the mirror, then bent forward quickly. The pain in her stomach became a sharp jab in her side. She straightened up, slowly this time. She gazed at her reflection. Yes, she was a pink-pink. Her freckles didn't even show. That's what happened when you took hot, hot showers. A sudden chill shook her. The room seemed so cold by contrast.

Kit was delighted to zip Sue into her dress. Now she felt good. Now she looked just right. Even her eyes looked extra bright and shiny. Was this what people meant when they said you had stars in your eyes? It was ridiculous to get so excited, so worked up over a mere party. If only Ellen and Cathy would be there. And Ricky and Chester. But no, there would be just The Crowd. Maxine, Laura, Judy, Dave, Mo . . . Sue hated Mo even though he seemed to be Dave's best friend. He wore his hair too long, his pants too low.

And there was an insolent air about him that made Sue want to slap his face. Oh well, he'd be with Judy. And Dave would be with her.

"Ready, Sue?" Mom poked her head around the door. "Dave's already here."

"In a second." Hurriedly Sue removed the bobby pins and brushed her hair. She applied her Pink Perfection lipstick in even, sure strokes, then dropped it into her purse. Kit held out Mom's most exclusive bottle of perfume, and after Sue dabbed some behind her ears and on her wrists, she put a drop or two on Kit. She turned slowly before the mirror and Mom. "Okay?"

"Lovely, dear."

Dave was waiting in the entrance hall as Sue descended the stairs with Mom, Kit, and Jay trailing her. She read the approval in his eyes as he helped her into her sweater.

"I'll pick you up at eleven," called Dad as she and Dave walked out the door.

"Thank you, sir." Dave reached for Sue's hand as they walked down the sidewalk. She felt so proud, walking along beside him. If only she didn't feel so . . . so tired.

Music blared from Judy's home when they arrived. The party was already in full swing. They stopped for a moment at the entrance to the rumpus room. The shades were drawn, and one small lamp made only a soft circle of light. It was hard to discern the other couples.

"You're the last here," greeted Maxine. "You look cute," she added.

"Sue always looks nice in that dress." Judy laughed. "Every time she wears it."

Sue flushed. The way Judy said it made it sound as though she wore the pink dress every day.

"It's my favorite," said Dave, unaware, apparently, that Judy's remark had been a cut, not a compliment. "Let's dance."

Sue dropped her sweater and purse on the table beside the davenport and slipped into Dave's arms. Someone had turned down the volume on the record player, and the music was slow and dreamy. They moved slowly, rhythmically around the floor. It felt so *right* to be dancing with Dave. Sue wondered how she could have been so nervous those few short weeks ago at the Peppermint Prom.

"How's my cutie-pie?" Dave murmured, and Sue knew he didn't mean Kit this time.

"Fine," she said. And she was fine, except for the nagging pain that had now turned into a jabbing one.

Occasionally she and Dave paused in their dancing to talk a moment or two with another couple. Sue noticed that Judy and Mo were dancing—if you could call it dancing—in the corner. She had her arms around his neck, and his were tight around her waist. They looked as though they were in a perpetual Hollywood embrace, and Sue felt embarrassed for them. She wondered what Judy's parents would say if they were to come in. But Judy apparently meant what she said when she'd announced they'd promised not to get in her hair. Sue knew that Mom and Dad would at least have been at the door at the party's start to meet and greet all the guests. She gave a mental shrug. At least, if this was what Judy meant by a super party, Sue could agree.

The room was getting hotter and stuffier by the moment. Sue wished someone would open another window or the door. Maybe she could ask Dave. But before she got the chance, someone put on a fast record and Dave swung her out onto the floor. In and out, back and forth they went. Dave grinned at her and winked. *He was proud of her.* Sue twirled under his arm and felt her pink dress swish around her knees. *This was really good.* Dave grasped both her hands and swung her to him. As she swung out again, a dagger of pain hit her side and she almost doubled over. She caught her breath sharply. "Let's sit down," she gasped, almost unable to straighten up.

"What's the matter?" Dave asked as she sank to the davenport.

"I don't know." Sue could feel beads of perspiration cold on her forehead. She felt scared. Never in her whole life had she felt so horrible.

"Do you want a Coke or something?"

Sue shuddered. Anything sweet would be terrible. "Water, maybe," she said.

As Dave moved across the room, Maxine sat down beside Sue. "Lend me your lipstick," she said. "I forgot mine."

Sue leaned forward. The pain eased up when she was leaning this way. She reached in her purse and handed the lipstick to Maxine. She was grateful Maxine didn't notice anything was wrong.

"Hey, two girls alone on a davenport? That'll never do. Move over, Maxine."

Sue looked up to see Mo standing before them. Maxine shifted over and Mo dropped between them. "Looks like this baby hasn't even gotten her lipstick messed yet." Mo put his arm across Sue's shoulder and pulled her toward him. "I'll fix that."

"No." Sue struggled from his grasp. *Where was Dave?*

"Judy followed Dave into the kitchen," Mo said, as if answering Sue's thoughts. "They'll be quite a while. Come on, give." He pulled her toward him again.

Sue pushed against him with her hands as hard as she could. She looked around the room frantically. The other couples had stopped dancing. All eyes were turned on her—and Mo.

"You're going to kiss me," Mo said through clenched teeth. He stood up and pulled Sue roughly to her feet. His grip on her arm hurt as he tried to pin it behind her back.

"No!" With every ounce of strength she could muster, Sue pulled away from him, and with her free hand she swung, catching him right across the face. She heard Maxine's startled gasp as Mo involuntarily let go.

The threat of nausea swept over her, and Sue knew with frantic certainty she had to get out, get away. She spun on her heel and ran from the room, out into the street. She had to get home—had to—had to. She had to reach Mom and Dad. They'd make everything all right. She ran on, her footsteps echoing strangely in her ears. The dagger of pain hit her again, and she almost stumbled. She caught herself and stopped, panting. The nausea hit her so strongly this time she could barely stagger over to the curb. Finally she tried to straighten up. She wiped at her mouth with the back of her hand. Maybe—if she took it slower—she could get home. As she turned to the sidewalk she heard footsteps pounding behind her.

"Sue. Sue, wait." Dave sounded frantic.

As he reached her side, Sue turned her head away from him. "Go away," she pleaded. "Just go away."

"Sue." Dave pulled her to a stop and she swayed. "Sue. I thought you were just angry. But you're sick. You're so white."

"Please." Sue's eyes and throat burned, and she was afraid she might be sick again. "Please, just leave me alone."

"Don't be a dope, Sue." Dave put his arm across her

back and held her as though he was trying to give her support. "Sit over on the steps of one of those houses, and I'll call your Dad."

Sue let herself be led. It felt good to sit down. And Dave's cardigan, which he slipped around her shoulders, felt warm and comforting.

"Stay there. I'll be right back," Dave commanded.

"Don't phone from Judy's," Sue begged.

"I won't," Dave promised. He took off at a run down the street and disappeared into the night.

Sue shifted her position until her back rested against the parapet. She closed her eyes so they wouldn't burn as much. Dave. He was wonderful. He didn't even seem to mind that she was ugly—and smelled. Sue shivered and drew his sweater closer around her.

"There she is."

Dave's voice made Sue jerk her eyes open. Had she dozed? Dad wasn't with him. Dave was getting out of a patrol car, with the officer right behind him.

The pain had eased up, and Sue walked almost comfortably between Dave and the officer to the car.

"Your young man gave me a scare," the officer said as he put the car in gear and drove off. "My car almost hit him."

"I had to stop you. I couldn't find a place to phone." Dave held Sue's hand tight in his. "She needed help."

Mom turned pale when she answered the door and saw

Sue standing between the policeman and Dave. "It's the flu, Mom," Sue explained. "I got these cramps in my side." Her voice broke and she felt the tears start down her cheeks.

And then—and then she was on the davenport with Mom fussing over her with cushions and a cold cloth for her head. And Dad—Dad was phoning.

"We're to take her to the hospital at once," Dad called in.

"Which one of us?" Mom asked. "We can't leave Kit and Jay alone."

"I'll stay," Dave offered. "I'll take care of the kids."

"Well——" Dad hesitated only a moment. "That's fine, son." The relief in his face was obvious. "Phone your folks and tell them you're here."

"I won't have to." Dave gave a derisive laugh. "Only Alison's home. She won't care."

"Better phone," Dad insisted. "We might be quite a while."

"If it makes you feel better," Dave promised. "But it isn't necessary."

"I go to the hospital for the flu? Just the flu?" Sue protested. But no one even bothered to listen to her. In a matter of minutes she was in the back seat of the car with Mom, and Dad was backing out of the driveway. Dave stood framed in the doorway.

"Wait," he called, a frantic urgency in his voice, and Dad stopped the car sharply. When Dave reached the car he opened the back door and leaned across Mom to Sue. He brushed his lips quickly across her forehead. "Good luck, Sue," he said. He backed out of the car, then, his face scarlet, and Dad took off.

Her first kiss. Sue snuggled deeper into the sweater—*his* sweater—that she was wearing, and the car swung around the corner, off toward the hospital.

14
Alibi

DR. JOHNSON WAS WAITING at the hospital when Sue arrived. "Causing a bit of excitement, eh?" he chided as she was whisked to the examining room. There the hustle and bustle would never make you think it was nighttime. It hurt to lie flat on the examining table, and Dr. Johnson's probing fingers hurt even more. He turned from Sue and picked up the phone.

"Dr. Johnson," he announced. "Prepare surgery for an appendectomy." He winked at Sue. "Just to be doubly sure," he said, "we'll have a blood count."

As he left, a nurse with a whole trayful of gadgets came in. The prick of the needle was a welcome diversion from the now steady, grinding pain in her side. An appendectomy? Things were happening so fast—too fast. Sue wished Mom and Dad would come into the room. Now the nurse with the tray left and an orderly and another nurse came in. They had a wheeled stretcher. Sue felt as though she were a box of groceries rather than a *person* as they transferred her. When she was rolled out into the hall, Sue looked frantically for Mom and Dad. It wasn't like them to leave her alone like this. She felt the tears push against her eyelids as she was wheeled into an elevator. Out of the elevator—down the hall—into a room—Mom and Dad were nowhere. Nowhere at all.

Sue tried to help herself as she was moved from the stretcher into the bed. "Relax, youngster," the nurse said. "We'll do the work." Sue just had time to notice there was another bed in the room—an occupied bed—when the curtains were drawn around her and another nurse came in to give a jab with another needle.

Now Sue could hear voices in the hall. Mom, Dad, Dr. Johnson. "Clearest case of appendicitis I've ever seen," Dr. Johnson said. Sue strained to hear Mom and Dad, but all she heard was a murmur of voices like a faraway river. Her eyelids felt heavy, and she struggled to stay awake. She was being wheeled out the door and into the hall again. This time Mom and Dad were there.

Mom kissed Sue on the cheek. "See you later, alligator," she said, recalling to Sue her very young days.

Dad leaned over, too, his eyes warm with love and concern. "We'll be right here, honey." His lips brushed hers.

"Okey-doke, artichoke," Sue murmured. She tried to smile but her mouth felt heavy. Down the hall—into the elevator—and now into a room where the lights were so bright they hurt her eyes. Dr. Johnson looked strange in his all-white costume.

"All set, sweetie-pie?" he asked.

Sue nodded. Dr. Johnson looked as though he might be smiling behind his mask. Now her arms—her legs—her whole body, in fact, seemed filled with a sort of lethargy. She didn't have enough energy to lift a finger. Once more she was moved, this time to the operating table. She was too tired and sleepy to even try to help. Sue closed her eyes, relaxing. Another needle . . .

She opened her eyes, shut them, and opened them again. The lights weren't quite as bright—or maybe she was just used to them. Dr. Johnson was holding her wrist.

"When—will—you—operate?" Sue forced herself to ask.

"It's all over with." Dr. Johnson laid her hand beside her. "You're in the recovery room."

Sue shook her head, trying to emerge from the cotton batting that seemed to envelope her. "Save it," she managed to say. "For Jay and Kit." And then she felt the cotton batting close in on her again.

"Say 'Good night,' Sue." Sue felt herself shaken. "Your Mother and Dad . . ." *Her nap. She must wake up from her nap and get ready for the party.*

"Rest, darling." Mom's cool voice came to her on little waves.

"Everything's fine, dear," Dad said. *What was he doing home from work so early?* Sue struggled to open her eyes, then let them stay closed. In a minute, just a little minute, she'd wake up. She'd tell Mom and Dad at dinner what a funny dream she'd had . . . about an operation. . . in just one minute . . .

The room was bright with sunshine when Sue opened her eyes. For a minute she didn't know where she was. Then she remembered. It hadn't been a dream. Her appendix was out. She turned her head to the sound of voices. A nurse was talking to someone over in the other bed. Sue let her eyelids drift shut, then opened them again. Now the nurse was by her bed.

"Well, good morning, sleepyhead. How do you feel?" The nurse's cheery voice and smile made Sue feel good.

"Fine," she said, and stirred in the bed. The pull of adhesive tape stopped her.

"Have you met your roommate?"

Sue shook her head.

"I'll make a formal introduction." The nurse looked over at the other bed. "Mrs. Mason," she said, "may I present Sue Stevens? And," she added, "I'm Mrs. Brown."

"Hi." Sue was surprised her voice sounded so far away. She tried again. This time her "hi" was louder.

As Sue and Mrs. Mason washed up for breakfast, Mrs. Mason kept up a steady chatter. She was young, Sue observed, and pretty. And she had twin daughters and a baby boy. Sue could meet the girls during visiting hours.

When the nurse had removed the basins, Mrs. Mason tuned in the portable radio by her bed. Music filled the room, and Sue felt herself slip off to sleep again. This time she awakened to Mrs. Brown's cheery announcement that it was breakfast time.

"I eat all that?" Sue eyed her tray in surprise.

"All you want." Mrs. Brown rolled up the bed until Sue was in a sitting position.

Sue sipped gingerly at her orange juice and tried a tentative taste of the cereal. Ordinarily she liked anything for breakfast. Now she felt as though she had fur in her mouth. She pushed the tray away and wished the nurse would come in soon. The food didn't even look good. She looked up expectantly as the door opened. It was Mom! Sue felt like smiling all over, it was so good to see her.

"Good morning, darling." Mom gave Sue a kiss. "I've brought your things." Sue watched as Mom put the hairbrush, toothbrush, bobby pins and bandana into the bedside table drawer. Mom hung bathrobe and slippers in the closet. She turned and smiled at Sue's neighbor.

"Oh, that's Mrs. Mason." Sue remembered to introduce.

Mom laughed. "We met last night."

"Gee, Mom"—Sue pushed back the covers quickly—
"I didn't even see my operation." Goodness. This time she
wasn't a pink-pink as Jay had called her. She was a violent
pink—from her knees to her chest. The dressing looked
large and important and very white. Jeepers!

"Our painted Indian." Mom laughed as she pulled the
covers up on Sue. "Do you hurt?"

Sue moved slightly. "Not unless I jerk, I guess," she said.

All too soon, it seemed to Sue, Mom was gone and she
was caught up in the hospital routine. Mostly, though, she
guessed she must have slept. There were a couple of shots,
of course. And Dr. Johnson came in to see her. In fact, it
seemed that every time she got to sleep, someone came
along and did something new to her.

Sue felt worn out by the time visiting hours were over
that afternoon. Mrs. Mason's twins were darling, but they
were so bouncy they made Sue nervous. What if one should
bump her? Mom was in for a few minutes with two weird
drawings done by Jay and Kit—their ideas on operations.
There'd even been the excitement of getting flowers. One
bouquet was from the Youngs—and the other was from
Mrs. Cannon. Dave, naturally, had told Mrs. Young. But
how had Mrs. Cannon known?

Now Sue relaxed against her pillows comfortably
and half asleep as usual, waiting for the evening's visit
with Dad. Her hands and face were washed and she felt
refreshed. She'd even made a stab at brushing her hair.

Tomorrow she'd put on lipstick. Mrs. Mason was reading a book, her radio turned down dreamy low. It felt so good, just to lie here, not even bothering to think.

She must have dozed off, for when she opened her eyes next, Sue saw Dad and Dave standing by her bed just as though some magician had made them appear. Oh no! Her hand flew to her face. Why, she didn't even have any lipstick on.

"Dave insisted on seeing the cause of his baby-sitting," Dad explained after he'd kissed her. "We're only to stay a few minutes."

"Here." Dave thrust a prettily wrapped package at her. "Alison said to bring it." Dave's face was an embarrassed red, and he looked as though he was on the defensive. "And I brought your purse, too," he added. "I picked it up at Judy's." He laid the purse on the table next to the bed.

Sue's fingers were all thumbs as she took off the package wrappings. She opened the box. "Ummmm, candy," she exclaimed. "It's beautiful." She offered the box to Dad and Dave.

"You first," Dave commanded. "You have to take the first piece."

Sue studied the box. All the candies were so big. She wasn't the least bit hungry. Especially for sweets. But Dave was so cute—and embarrassed. She finally selected a piece, and then almost laughed as Dave took three and Dad two.

"Hey." Dave sounded angry. "Hey, where's our bracelet?"

Sue looked at her arm. The bracelet. What had happened to it? She poked her thoughts back through the cloud of this morning and last night. Finally she shook her head. "I don't know," she said. "I don't remember."

"It's in your drawer in an envelope," Dad stated. "The nurse put it there last night."

Dave rummaged through the drawer, past her toothpaste and brush, past the bandana, and then with a triumphant grin he pulled forth the envelope. "Here," he said as he ripped it open and took out the bracelet. He fastened it around her wrist. "Now we're steadies again."

Sue didn't know why, but she suddenly remembered Dave's kiss. She could feel herself blush. Maybe Dave was remembering, too, because he looked away, embarrassed. An awkward silence seemed to fill Sue's half of the room. Dad cleared his throat.

"Well, babykin," he said. "Mom said only a couple of minutes to visit. We'd better leave." The flowers caught his attention. "Hmmmmm, yours?" he asked.

Sue nodded. "Oh, Dave," she said, "the baby roses are from Alison. Please, please thank her." She pointed to the other flowers. "These," she said, "are from Mrs. Cannon. How did she know?"

Dad smiled. "Seems that she saw you and Dave and the police car last night."

"Oh." Sue wished the flowers were out of sight. Snoopy Mrs. Cannon was at it again.

Dad patted Sue's hand. "We really have to go." He reached in his coat pocket and drew out the evening paper. "Something to read," he said as he handed it to Sue.

The headlines caught her eye as she opened it. "Vandals Invade, Wreck Home" she read aloud. "Police Suspect Teen-Agers." Her eyes widened. This sounded exciting.

"*Kids*," exclaimed Dad, his voice angry. "It must have been kids. Imagine anyone doing a thing like that!"

"Wait, let me read," begged Sue. Her eyes scanned the column. Mr. and Mrs. James Driscoll of 1504 Central Avenue had returned home from a theater party about midnight to find that someone—or more likely a group—had broken into their home, slashed furniture, smashed the television, drawn with lipstick on the walls, and——

"Idiots! Delinquents!" Dad's anger made his voice extra loud.

"Shhh." Sue looked at Dave, embarrassed at Dad's outburst. But Dave—Dave averted his eyes quickly, and Sue saw that his knuckles were white as he gripped the end of the bed. Dave—*scared*? But why? Panic closed Sue's ears as Dad continued on his tirade . . . 1504 *Central Avenue—that must be—it was—just about around the corner from Judy's. And Dave had brought her purse.*

About midnight, the paper said. *How long do appendectomies take?*

Sue fought for casualness. She folded the paper carefully, deliberately, and tucked it under her pillow. "I'll read it later," she told her father. She looked at Dave. "Uh, Dave," she said—yes, her voice was cool, calm and collected—"did you get stuck baby-sitting long? At my house last night, I mean?"

"Huh?" Dave seemed to have to grab his thoughts from someplace else and come back to the room. "Oh—not too long."

"Not too long but long enough," Dad amended. "I don't guess we reached home before midnight. And there were Jay and Dave, waiting."

"Jay?"

"He woke up," Dave explained. "And when he saw me he was full of questions. So I let him stay up. Seemed better that way."

"Then you were at my house—with Jay—until midnight?" Sue felt as though she was prying, but she had to know.

"More like one o'clock." Dad interrupted again. "Mom made the boys hot chocolate, she and I had coffee, and we all had cinnamon toast."

"A party—and I wasn't invited." Sue pretended to feel hurt, but she felt like singing. Dave was clear. He was clear. Maybe the others—but—Dave was in the clear.

"Look kitten, we've got to run." Dad leaned over and kissed Sue good night. "And I'm sorry if I embarrassed you with my loud talk. I just hate destruction for its own sake. I just can't——"

"That's okay, Dad," Sue interrupted. She held out her hand to Dave.

"See you, Sue," Dave said as he patted her hand clumsily. But his eyes were still troubled.

When the two had left, Sue reread the paper. That's what they meant—the Jay Dees—when they'd said "a different party."

It must have been they—right around the corner from Judy's—and Dave knew something about it, she could tell by the change that came over him when she opened the paper.

What if she hadn't gotten sick—no doubt they would have tried to involve her—and Dave. She'd never have thought it would be lucky to get sick—but if it *was* the Jay Dees, she was lucky this time. She and Dave both had an alibi—a perfect one. Even the police could vouch for them. The paper said theft was not a motive—the only item missing was brass knuckles from Mr. Driscoll's collection of weapons. As for clues, there was only one—and not a good one at that. Someone had dropped a lipstick, one that was a popular brand. Sue's heart pounded as she reached for her purse. Her lipstick wasn't there—she'd loaned it to Maxine. Was the one picked up by the police *Pink Perfection*?

15

Back Home

JUST WHEN SUE FELT accustomed to the hospital routine, she was whisked home. Only three days for an appendectomy! She could hardly believe her ears when Dr. Johnson came into the room, changed the dressing, and said. "Come to my office in a week for those stitches. And take it easy at home."

Sue felt slightly cheated. Today was the first day she could really expect visitors. Tonight, that is. Because today, being Monday, was the first chance most of her friends had of learning she'd even had an operation. To be so important for such a short while! Even the dressing was an insignificant patch compared to the large, impressive square of gauze she'd worn down from surgery. Oh well, it would be good to get home. Sue bid her farewells to the nurses and Mrs. Mason and sat in the wheel chair with as much regal aplomb as she could muster. Hall, elevator, and then down the ramp to the waiting car. At least Mom treated her as though she was something fragile and delicate.

The day was one of those extra-hot spring days that just scream for a bathing suit and a swimming pool. Even with a fan going full blast, her bedroom seemed uncomfortably warm when Sue finally edged into bed. Or maybe it was just warm after the hard work of climbing the stairs.

"Where are Jay and Kit?" Sue leaned forward so Mom could give the pillows an extra fluffing.

"Jay's in school, dear, and Kit's at a neighbor's."

Sue glanced at her clock. How could it still be so early when the day felt as though it should soon be over? She settled herself with distaste in her bed. Personally, she was getting fed up with beds. Although leaning back against the pillows was comfortable.

Mother came into the room, carrying a washcloth. She handed it to Sue. "Pat your face, darling," she said. "You'll soon be more comfortable."

The cloth did feel good, coolly damp with a fresh eau de cologne odor to it.

"Now try to rest awhile." Mom took the cloth from Sue and drew the curtains.

Sue watched Mom pull the door shut with a feeling of regret. It was so "alone" in her bedroom. Rest! That was a boring idea. But Mother was a sweetie. So were Dad and

Jay and Kit—and Dave. But Dave hadn't been to see her yesterday. Why? Was he being—*questioned?* Because of that house? In yesterday's paper there had been only the briefest mention of the vandalism. "Authorities were still investigating."

The house was unnaturally quiet. How could Mom stand it—being alone all day like this? Sue switched on her radio, and the music was a welcome diversion. At least it broke the vacuum. Still, she was more than ready when she heard the front door open with a bang and Jay and Kit stormed up the stairs with the quietness of a herd of elephants.

"Did it hurt?" Kit asked.

"Let's see," begged Jay.

Sue showed off her quite small bandage. But they hadn't seen the original and were quite impressed.

The two bounced around on her bed, showing their delight in seeing Sue again. She was afraid they were going to bump into her side, and when they suddenly started squabbling she almost missed the protective routine of the hospital and was relieved when Mom took them downstairs. She relaxed again to the music of her radio and was shocked when Dad appeared at her door bearing her supper tray. She'd slept—how many hours?

"Stay with me," Sue begged.

"We'll all eat up here," Dad promised.

Sue beamed as she watched her family attack the delicious food Mom served. Gee, it was wonderful to be home. Dad must have thought so too.

"All noses accounted for," he said. "All safe and sound under one roof."

Getting Kit and Jay to bed that night was a real ordeal. Sue didn't envy Dad and Mom. Mainly it was because the phone and doorbell kept ringing. Dad wore such a broad, happy grin whenever he reported a message to Sue.

And her first visitors! Sue could hardly believe her eyes when Cathy and Ellen walked into her room bearing a gift-wrapped record. The three of them talked and giggled and had as much fun as they'd had in their grade school days. They'd been gone only a few minutes when Dad announced Maxine. She, too, had a gift in hand. Sue tore off the exquisite wrapping and opened the box. She looked up quickly at Maxine, but Maxine sat with eyes averted.

Sue's hand shook as she held the jeweled lipstick case. *Was this an admission—of guilt?* This was much more exclusive than Pink Perfection. The shade of lipstick was a delicate rose. Mom would approve. "Thank you, Maxine," Sue said. "It's beautiful."

"Mom thought it was pretty," Maxine answered. "I—I——" her voice faltered. "I guess I must have lost yours," she ended lamely.

Sue hesitated. Should she mention Judy's party? Maxine

must have read her thoughts, because she launched feverishly into a discourse on school as if she didn't want Sue to talk.

Ask me no questions and I'll tell you no lies. Was that the attitude Maxine was taking? Sue found conversation difficult. They were both skirting Judy's party—and Judy and Laura—carefully. Relief surged through Sue when Dad called up that more visitors were on their way. After all, you couldn't keep talking about nothing forever.

Maxine's relief showed in her face. She stood up quickly. "I'll see you," she said. "I've lots of homework tonight." Her eyes widened in surprise as she met Sue's newest guests at the bedroom door. "You!" she exclaimed, and stepped aside to let Ricky and Chester enter the room. She beat a hasty retreat down the stairs.

"You!" Sue almost echoed. Ricky and Chester were guests she hadn't expected at all.

The boys stood there, uncomfortable, ill at ease. Because they were in a girl's bedroom, Sue wondered, or because they hadn't wanted to come and their mothers made them.

Ricky plunked the couple of books he'd been carrying on Sue's bed. "Here," he said. "I picked up the rest of your books." He drew a piece of paper out of his pocket and handed it to Sue. "And here are your assignments for the week."

Ever-thoughtful, thorough Rick. He took school so seriously. Sue wasn't too sure she was grateful for having her homework brought to her.

"Show her the other stuff," demanded Chester.

Ricky reached into another pocket and brought out a jumbled mess of papers of assorted sizes. "The kids in your home room wrote you notes," he explained. He handed them to Sue.

Sue smoothed out the papers. "Let's read them now," she suggested.

The boys propped themselves on either side of Sue as they all read together. Some of the letters were hard to decipher. Some were boring. Others were downright hysterical. She laughed until her stitches actually hurt.

"Some comedians," chuckled Rick.

"Just a couple of cards!"

At the sneering voice the three of them looked up, startled. Dave was leaning against the door, watching them. His eyes looked angry, and Sue felt her face flush. Ricky and Chester jumped up.

"Hi, Dave." Sue was angry with herself for feeling embarrassed. There was no reason, no reason at all.

"Thought you might be lonesome." Dave's mouth was a straight, hard line. "My mistake." He turned as though ready to leave.

"Wait, Dave," Sue pleaded.

"We were leaving anyhow," Ricky said. Chester had a closed, scared look on his face.

"Don't let me stop you." Dave stepped inside the doorway and leaned against the wall as if—as if he didn't want to be *contaminated* by the other two.

"David Young!"

"Forget it, Sue. We were leaving anyway." Ricky's smile was gentle and understanding. "Let's go, Chester."

Chester hurried after Ricky to the door with the alacrity of a scared jack rabbit.

Ricky gave Sue a friendly salute. "See you later, kid."

"Thank you," Sue called belatedly as she heard the two boys thump inelegantly down the stairs. "Thanks for the books and letters."

Dave came across the room and seated himself on Sue's bed. "This is better," he said. He reached for Sue's hand.

How could he change moods so quickly? Sue withdrew her hand from his clasp. "You were rude," she said. Her anger showed in her voice.

"Rude—to those drips?"

"They're my friends."

"Friends!" Dave stood up, his eyes angry again. "I thought," he said slowly, "that going steady meant you didn't cheat."

"Cheat!" Sue felt her chin jut out. "I don't cheat." She almost hissed the word. "Ricky and Chester are friends. They've been my friends since—for years and years. They're *friends,*" she emphasized. "Not *boy* friends."

"They're jerks, if that's the kind of friends you want."

"So my friends are jerks!" Sue's voice shook, she was so furious. "But your friends—they are strictly *choice*, I suppose. Judy, Laura, Mo. They are simply wonderful."

"Okay, Sue." Dave's voice had the burning quality of dry ice. "Don't forget, two can play your game. You've asked for it." He strode to the door. "See you—maybe."

Sue stared with unbelieving eyes at the vacated doorway. Dave. How could he leave like that! How could he be so stupidly misunderstanding. He was making a mountain out of a molehill. He wasn't even trying to see things straight. *Two can play the game.* What did he mean by that? That he'd give Judy a rush now? How could he be so unreasonable? Hadn't he ever heard of just plain *friends?* Sue felt the tears rush to her eyes as she fingered her bracelet—*his* bracelet. At least he'd have to be by to get it if he meant they were breaking up. Maybe she could explain better then.

There were no more guests that night. Sue was glad She felt depressed and exhausted. She couldn't have been fun to visit. When Mom came to help Sue complete her toiletries for the night, her eyes were questioning.

"What in the world is the matter with Dave?" she asked. "He actually stormed out of the house."

"He didn't like Ricky and Chester being here," Sue said simply.

"Too bad about that young man. Competition never hurt anyone."

Dave is hurt by it, Sue wanted to say, but she stayed silent. It felt good just to relax and be babied.

Mom gave Sue a tiny dinner bell as she and Dad said their good nights. "Ring if you need anything, darling," she told Sue.

Sue lay in the cool darkness. Two tears rolled down her cheeks. She brushed them away. The day had been so good—and so bad. She reached over to turn off the muted music on the radio. Her hand touched the box Maxine had brought. Quickly, decisively she leaned on her elbow and put the gift in the drawer. She shut it firmly. *That* she would *not* think about. She rested her cheek against the bracelet. If only Dave would be *sweet* again!

16

The Warning

BEFORE THE WEEK OF her convalescence was over, Sue welcomed the chance to work at her schoolbooks. At least it was something to do. Days literally dragged. Mom, Jay, Kit, Dad, everyone had his own pattern of activities, and even though the family *tried*, there weren't too many spare hours to give to Sue.

Visitors, after that first day, dwindled down to three. Cathy, Ellen, Maxine. That was *it*. And their visits were certainly nothing you could call long. Sue was glad Mom had set up some knitting for her to do. She worked carefully on the tiny woolly hat. Alison would like it for the new baby-to-be even if Sue never saw Dave again.

Mom and Dad had openly wondered at first why Dave didn't come by. Then, blessedly, they dropped the subject. Sue was glad. Dave was disciplining her, she hoped, or was he now completely uninterested?

Maxine brought up the subject of Dave one shattering afternoon. "How come you're still wearing Dave's bracelet?" she asked Sue. "I thought Judy'd have it by now."

Sue shot a startled look at Maxine.

"He's with The Crowd at lunch time," Maxine explained. "And Judy's with Dave as much as she is with Mo now."

After Maxine left, Sue took off the bracelet and put it in the drawer. If Dave should come by to collect it, he'd find her most unconcerned.

Eventually, of course, the day rolled around when Sue went to Dr. Johnson's office to have the stitches removed. She tensed as she lay on the examination table. This might hurt. But it didn't, not at all.

"All set," Dr. Johnson said as he helped Sue down from the table. "School tomorrow."

Sue felt the excitement bubble within her like a growing thing. *Back to school.* And then she realized Dr. Johnson was talking to her. "Pick up your excuse from the nurse," he said. "No physical education for a month. And remember," he continued, while Sue listened to him aghast, "no swimming, jumping, skipping, hopping, running, dancing, or any exerting exercise of any kind for a month."

A *month!* Why, she might as well be an Egyptian mummy. She'd be able to have no fun at all. This was terrible! All work and no play would surely make her a very dull girl.

Sue prepared for school the next morning very carefully.

If she was going to have to be a delicate hothouse plant, she might as well *look* like one. But her reflection in the mirror was a disgustingly healthy one. She puzzled for a time over what to do with Dave's bracelet. She couldn't wear it after what Maxine said. But should she take it—in case Dave asked for it back? Or should she pretend great indifference and say something like "Your bracelet? Oh. I'd forgotten all about it. It must be home in my drawer." Sue finally slipped the bracelet in her purse. She'd be a good scout. She'd be prepared.

No walk to school in the warm spring sunshine today. Dr. Johnson wasn't the only one who'd imposed rules. Mom and Dad had a few of their own. Mom would chauffeur Sue to and from school the first week. And there would be no orchestra.

Thanks to Mom's habit of trying to get as many last-minute chores done as possible, Sue arrived at school just as the warning bell rang. By the time she cleared with the attendance office, classes had started.

As she opened the door to her home room, her fellow students *and* Mr. Henderson gave her a rousing "welcome back." Sue felt herself blush with pleasure as she took her seat. The class settled down to work in just a couple of minutes, and Sue was appalled at how behind she was, even with the homework she'd done during her absence. How could they have raced through so much!

Sue was grateful when Mr. Henderson asked her to stay in during recess so he could explain some of the work. For some reason she felt as though she'd lived in a cocoon for the last week and she wasn't ready to emerge. Now that she was friendly again with Cathy and Ellen, she wanted to stay that way. How could she bridge the gap between them and the Jay Dees? Or was she even wanted as a Jay Dee any longer? That was a pleasant thought—to vision herself *out* of The Crowd. Lunch time arrived with such deadly certainty she was reminded of the poem Jay had written when school started. "September," he'd scrawled. "I'm glad it's here. It always comes this time of the year."

Students crowded through the doors and out into the yard. Sue picked up her lunch bag and joined the throng. She saw Cathy in the distance and waved. Cathy waved back gaily, then continued on her way, catching up to Ellen. Why, they were going to ignore her!

Sue broke away from the general noise and confusion and walked over to the low brick wall. Perhaps Cathy and Ellen would be over in a minute. She sat alone and lonely and opened her lunch bag. Maxine and the other Jay Dees were over near the basketball courts, laughing and chatting with a group of boys. Dave was with them. She bit into her sandwich and chewed it slowly. If only she could swallow past the lump in her throat. She saw Maxine look over in her direction. This time Sue was waving at no one. Maxine walked over to Sue, munching an apple.

"Hi, Sue." Maxine leaned against the wall. "Judy says come on over."

A request or demand, Sue wondered briefly. She started to shake her head, then decided against it. Might as well go over. Might as well face Judy and Dave *now*. She clutched her purse tight against her and stood up. But now The Crowd seemed to be drifting to where she and Maxine were. Sue sat down again.

"Hi, Sue."

How could any person express such scorn, such triumph in a mere two words! Sue acknowledged the greeting as her gaze went past Judy to Dave. His face was set and hard as he pushed forward toward her.

"Where is it?" he demanded roughly. "Where's the bracelet?"

Sue fumbled in her purse. Her fingers touched the cool silver links. How horribly humiliating to return a bracelet like this—before everyone. Had it been planned this way? She thrust it at Dave as though it might burn her fingers. "Here," she said through clenched teeth. "Take it."

"Ooooooh." Judy's coo was an ecstatic sigh as she reached for the bracelet. "Let me see, Dave."

"Skip it." Dave jammed the bracelet into his pocket. He turned on his heel and shouldered his way quickly through the group.

Sue tore her gaze from Dave's retreating back to look at Judy. Why, she was as humiliated as Sue! Her face was scarlet. She glared at Sue with eyes that blazed with pure, undiluted hatred.

"Come on, gang." Judy jerked her head in the direction of the basketball courts. "We've things to discuss."

Maxine gave Sue a despairing look as she meekly followed in Judy's wake. What if *she* should decide to go along, too, Sue wondered. After all she *was* part of the gang. She *was* a Jay Dee. There was no reason why Judy should push her around. Sue stood up, then sat down again. It wasn't worth the effort. She crumbled up the lunch bag beside her. Too bad she wasn't hungry today.

"Sue?"

Sue looked up to see Mr. Henderson standing before her. "Mr. Mack would like to see you—now."

Sue welcomed the chance to leave the yard. She walked quickly to the office.

Mr. Mack looked up as Sue stood in the doorway. He looked so *welcoming,* "Sit down, Sue." He motioned to a chair. "It's good to have you back."

Here, in the security of Mr. Mack's office, it was good to be back.

"Sue,"—Mr. Mack's fingers drummed lightly on the edge of his desk—"we have a problem here at Taft that I think you can help."

Sue's spirits perked up. To be needed—just a little?

"What do you know about the Driscoll home?"

Sue raised startled eyes to Mr. Mack's face. The Driscoll

home . . . her lipstick. She dropped her gaze quickly. Had her suspicions shown in her eyes? "I—I read about it," she said slowly.

"I didn't think you knew anything about it." Mr. Henderson's voice was pleased. "But I had to make sure."

Sue let out her breath slowly, evenly. So her thoughts hadn't been readable. She waited for Mr. Mack to continue.

"Graduation will be here soon—and then summer vacation." Mr. Mack paused. He seemed to be groping for the right words. "Vandalism, such as that which took place at the Driscoll home, is a new thing in our community. It has to stop before it gains momentum. It has to stop *before* our school term ends. Or someone might be hurt." He looked at Sue somberly, and she wondered if she was supposed to say something.

"The police are sure the culprits are Taft students. Certain ones are already under their—ah—watchful eyes."

Sue held her breath. Mr. Mack was warning—*her?* He leaned across the desk confidentially. "You can help by telling us, Sue."

"Telling you?"

"Letting us know if and when any future acts are contemplated."

"You—you think I'm a *vandal?*"

"If we did, we'd hardly call you in like this. But you might hear of something."

For a moment Sue had a wild desire to tell her suspicions.

Judy had it coming to her. Revenge would be sweet. Or would it? Could she, Susan Stevens, live with herself if her suspicions were wrong? Mr. Mack was asking her to be a second Mrs. Cannon again. He was asking her to be an informer. Sue studied her hands as she spoke. "I won't hear anything, Mr. Mack," she said slowly. "And if I did, I wouldn't tell."

"Sue, Sue." Mr. Mack stood up, and Sue noticed how weary he looked. "I'm sorry I failed. I'm sorry I didn't make my point. Can't you see you'd be *helping*? Not just us, but the others. The ones who do these things."

Sue didn't answer. There was no answer. She watched Mr. Mack walk over to the door. She stood up and followed him. She was being dismissed.

"Just remember, Sue, we're here to help." Mr. Mack sighed, and Sue thought his shoulders sagged. "If you ever need us, come running. And remember, too, your parents are proud of you and have faith in you. Don't let them down."

"I'll remember."

"Thank you." Mr. Mack gave Sue's shoulder a pat. "Hurry to class now. You're late, but you won't need a corridor pass. Your teacher knows you've been with me."

School was finally over for the day. What a dismal first day back. Dave . . . Mr. Mack . . . Judy . . . Cathy . . . Ellen . . . Sue walked slowly down the corridor to meet Mom at the south entrance. Oh, to get in the car.

"Here we are, Sue." Jay waved wildly from the car window.

She quickened her steps. The family chariot had never looked so good. She passed her books through the window to Jay, opened the door, and climbed in beside him. She sank back comfortably as Mom switched on the ignition. Mom was just about to pull away from the curb when Kit jerked the door open and bounded out onto the sidewalk.

"Dave, Dave," she screamed. "Here we are."

"Get *in*," Sue begged. "Keep quiet, Kit."

Kit didn't bother to listen. She ran up the walk to where Dave, Mo, Judy, Laura, and Maxine were talking together. She took Dave's hand and pulled him toward the car, and Sue huddled down in the corner, trying to make herself as small as possible.

"Kit says I may have a ride, Mrs. Stevens." Dave opened the door to the front seat. "Okay?"

"Hop in."

Sue wished she had the nerve to look back to see Judy's expression as Mom drove off.

"Sit up, Sue," Jay demanded. "You're crowding me."

Sue straightened up, miserably embarrassed, but Dave ignored her completely.

"Mind if I ride home with you?" he asked Mom.

"We'll even give you cookies and milk," Kit promised, without waiting for Mom to reply. Sue gritted her teeth. How could Kit calmly *bribe* him like that.

When Mom pulled into the driveway, Dave hopped out of the car quickly. He opened the back door. "I'll carry your books," he said pleasantly, as if nothing had ever happened.

Sue followed him wordlessly into the house.

"Now you sit down, young lady," Mother ordered. "You must be tired."

"I'll get the cookies," Jay volunteered.

"No, me." Kit pushed past her brother and hurried to the kitchen.

Sue sat on the davenport and wondered what in the world to say to Dave. Had he just come along to return her harmonica? He'd better hurry up if he was, because wandering around the room as he was doing, pretending to study the pictures, was just plain silly. He turned suddenly and faced her.

"What did you give it back for?" he demanded.

"You asked for it."

"No I didn't. I asked where it was. You weren't wearing it. Why?"

Sue frowned. Now Dave was trying to make everything sound like her fault. "They said you're going with Judy," she told him. "Besides, you didn't even call all week."

"I know." Dave gave Sue a lopsided grin. "I was being stupid, I guess. I was mad." He dropped on the davenport beside her. "Want it back?" He reached in his pocket and pulled out the bracelet, his eyes pleading.

Sue felt her irritations of the day melt away. "Yes," she said. She held out her arm and watched as Dave fastened the clasp.

"Now leave it be," he commanded. "You're so on again, off again. Relax." He gave the bracelet a final pat. "Guess I'll get going so you can rest," he added. "You look terrible."

"Thanks."

"That's all right. Just see you don't give it back again."

Sue giggled. "I wasn't thanking you for the bracelet. I was thanking you for your lovely compliments. Saying I look terrible."

"Aw, Sue." Dave's voice was suddenly soft and he cupped her chin in his hand and tilted up her face. "You know what I mean. Tired-terrible. Not terrible-terrible. Don't tease." He cuffed her chin gently with his fist. "Now take it easy." He walked to the front door. "Good-by, Mrs. Stevens," he called. "I've got to be going."

"Hey, wait." Jay tore into the room, both hands filled with cookies. "I brought us something. And Kit's bringing some pop."

"No pop today," Dave said as he took a cookie. "But I'll have one of these for the road."

Sue watched out the window as Dave sauntered down the walk. He was cute. And sometimes he was as sweet and lovable as Jay and Kit. Sometimes? Most of the time. She took the cookie Jay handed her and nibbled on it, savoring its spicy crispness. The late spring sunshine seeped through the windows and she basked in it, letting its warmth make her drowsy. Even the glass of orange soda Kit brought in didn't rouse her from just relaxing. Dimly she heard the phone ring, heard Jay answer it and say. "It's for Sue, Mom." But she didn't bother opening her eyes. And then, somehow, Dad was home and it was dinnertime.

"Maxine phoned," Mom said as she served Sue the vegetables. "There's a Jay Dee meeting tonight. I told her you couldn't go."

"Good." Sue picked up her fork and knife. Judy . . . Laura . . . Mo . . . the Jay Dees . . . why, they couldn't bother her. She was Sue Stevens, at peace with the world. Even Mr. Mack's warning wasn't important. The bracelet clinked pleasantly against the side of her plate as Sue cut into the chop.

17

Meeting Called to Order

THE NEXT TWO WEEKS were work-packed, yet they literally flew by. The fact that Sue's grades had slid back prior to her stay at the hospital meant she had to work that much harder to catch up with the class. And then the students were smack-bang into preparations for the big social studies test that was a state requirement. Laws, amendments, duties of departments, and names, names, names had whirled through her mind until she could barely relegate them to their categories. The times Dave had come over—and they were quite few—Dad had quizzed the two of them. Sue had been amazed Dave was so bright. He was much smarter than she. Dad had looked as though he thoroughly enjoyed his test periods. Oh well, now the exam was over. Everyone could relax. All she had to do right now was prepare for a meeting of the Jay Dees.

"What do you do at meetings?" Mom asked as she slathered inch-thick whipped cream on chocolate layers.

That's the question Sue had asked Maxine just today. She gave Mom Maxine's answer. "Mostly talk and listen to records."

"Sounds rather dull," Mom objected. "Don't you think you should do something philanthropic at club meetings?"

Sue looked at Mom with alarm. Neither Mom nor Dad approved of "idle hands." But she, Sue, was the newest member in the club. Actually, she'd never been to a Jay Dee meeting except for initiation. Sue grimaced as she recalled *that* night. "Look, Mom," she explained as lightly as she could. "Since I'm just beginning, maybe we'd better have things like they usually are."

"Hmmmmmmmm." Mom sounded as though she were deep in thought as she gave a final swirl to the top coating of cream. She sprinkled on some chocolate shavings and eyed the result with a critical expression. "Think they'll like it?"

"Oh, Mom." Sue gave her mother a quick hug. "We've never had such good refreshments."

Mom took the cake and placed it carefully on a shelf in the refrigerator. "We'll have ice cream and pink lemonade," she said. "That should fill them. But I still think just sitting is dull."

Sue pretended she hadn't heard. Now was not the time

to get into a discussion on the evils of idleness. This meeting had to be just perfect. Actually, being a Jay Dee these past two weeks had been just about perfect, too. For some reason, the girls were extra friendly. Sue knew Judy didn't like her, but the animosity had been well hidden. Lunch hours had been fun since that first horrible day back. Talking about nothing in particular had been relaxing. She'd seen Cathy and Ellen with Ricky and Chester, and even the fact that they weren't particularly friendly didn't bother her. Oh, Ricky always gave her a big smile and cheerful hello. But the others . . . Seeing Chester always reminded Sue of his Sunday suit. But she never asked Dave about it again.

"Can Kit and I come to the party?" Jay poked his head into the kitchen as Sue arranged a bowl of white lilac for the play room. "We'll be good."

"Huh uh." Sue was emphatic. "But I'll save you some cake," she promised.

"Is Dave coming?" Kit asked.

"It's a girl meeting," Sue explained. "He can't come."

What would Dave be doing tonight, Sue wondered. She pushed the teacart into the kitchen to arrange the plates, napkins, and glasses. Maybe he'd stay home with Alison again—if his Dad was going out. That had been the pattern of Dave's home life anyway. Because Alison hadn't been feeling too well the last week. It wouldn't be long before Sue would be presenting her with the woolly hat.

Sue pushed the teacart into the playroom and then stood back and admired the effect. Everything looked just lovely. If only the evening could be lovely too.

Supper was a hurried affair that night, with Sue whisking the dishes off the table almost before the last bite had been taken. She was just drying the last one when the doorbell rang and the first girl arrived. Within five minutes they were all there. They stood around the living room awkwardly while Sue completed the introductions her parents insisted upon. Then she led them into the playroom while Mom ushered Kit and Jay upstairs and Dad settled down with his paper and pipe.

"Don't forget to save some cake," Kit and Jay yelled down the stairs.

Sue didn't bother to answer as Judy settled herself in the chair of honor. Judy looked as though there were important doings underfoot.

"We'll have the minutes, Laura," Judy announced importantly.

As Laura read the brief report, Sue decided she'd missed absolutely nothing with her absences.

Laura picked up a piece of paper. "I'll read the treasurer's report," she said. She scanned the paper. "You owe three dollars, Sue."

"Three dollars?" Sue heard her own voice squeak its surprise. Why, that was more than the whole treasury held.

"It's a privilege to be a Jay Dee. You've abused that privilege by not coming to meetings, so you have to pay a fine."

"I don't have three dollars."

"Get it or else." Judy's voice was flat, authoritative. "Maybe Dave could pay for you," she added.

"I wouldn't ask Dave." Sue's voice showed her scorn.

Judy shrugged. "I don't care how you get it, just get it." She turned to the other girls. "Maxine will have our next meeting," she said. "A party. Right?"

Maxine nodded.

"And it's to be some party. Right?" Judy repeated the word.

Maxine giggled nervously as she glanced first at Judy, then down at her feet.

"Don't worry, Maxine. I've cased the street with Mo. It'll be the greatest."

Sue felt her scalp prickle. "What do you mean, 'you cased the street'?"

"You'll see." Judy's smile seemed almost sinister. "And you won't have an appendix to take you home this time, either."

Was this a *warning* that Mr. Mack would like to hear? Or was Judy just going through her usual line of chatter because she knew it made Sue nervous?

"Meeting adjourned." Judy banged her gavel.

"Records, Sue, where are your records?" Laura asked.

Sue switched on her record player as her mother walked in. Sue looked at the box Mom held in her hands and her heart sank.

"Just had an idea, girls," Mom said in her cheeriest voice—the one she reserved for Jay and Kit when she wanted them to do something they didn't want to do. "Sue said you just listened to records for your meetings, so I thought you could work with your hands while you enjoyed them." She set the box on the table and spread out thicknesses of felt. "Beanbags," she announced. "For the Co-operative Nursery."

"Beanbags!" Judy sounded as startled as if Mom announced a visitor from Mars.

"Yes." Mom laid a fish pattern on black felt and beckoned to Laura. "Here, you may start."

Sue swallowed. Mom had that Carrie Nation look in her eyes, and when she had that look there was no stopping her. Laura must have recognized the expression, too, for she came over to the table quite willingly and picked up the scissors.

In a matter of minutes the girls were busily cutting out their patterns, and Mom set up the portable sewing machine. "You girls have all sewn in school," she said, "and this is very simple."

"Fins and eyes?" Maxine asked.

"As gay as gay can be," Mom answered.

In spite of themselves, Sue thought, the girls were enjoying the fishy evening. She put on a fresh selection of records.

"I'll get the cake and see about beans," Mom said as the first girl finished her stint at the machine and another girl took her place.

"Is your mother always a do-gooder?" Judy asked, sarcasm dripping from her voice.

"I think it's a cute idea," Laura protested, and Sue shot her a grateful look.

"It's wonderful." Judy's face darkened, and Sue caught the venom in the look that darted her way. "So good you can improve Jay Dee routine, Sue. You must have thought of this project for hours."

Sue started to protest. This was strictly Mom's idea. But that would put Mom in a sort of "bossy" light. And no one—especially Judy—was going to criticize *her* family. "Could be," she answered with forced gaiety.

Judy appeared to be gathering her forces for another outburst when Mom returned with the cake and Dad followed with pitchers of lemonade. As Dad poured, Mom left the room again and returned this time with the beans.

In between gobbles of the cake, the girls stuffed their felt fish. And when the last crumb of cake was gone, the last drop drained from the lemonade pitchers, the last beanbag was finished too. Judy, Sue noticed, had declined to make a beanbag.

"We might have time for a quick game of charades," Dad ventured. "I loved it when I was a kid." He divided the group into teams. "Bet you can think of hard things to portray," he told Judy. "You look like an intelligent girl. How about starting things off?"

Sue almost laughed at the way Judy preened under the compliment. "We'll take songs," Judy announced, and she and her team went into a huddle.

The girls threw themselves wholeheartedly into the game, and Sue found even she was relaxing and having fun. All too soon the first parent came to collect his daughter, and, as quickly as the girls had arrived, the house now became empty.

"A nice group of youngsters," Dad said as he helped Sue clean up the debris in the room while Mom whipped out the vacuum. "That Judy is a born actress, too."

Sue was glad the hum of the vacuum made talking difficult. But she resented the way Dad seemed to be fooled by Judy's airs. Judy, the threatener, Judy the know-all, Judy, the girl who had whispered gaily as she left. "Remember the fine." And before Sue could say a word, she'd leaned over and whispered, "Know where Dave was tonight? Read tomorrow's paper."

Darn that Judy anyway. Now she'd started Sue worrying again. What had she meant? Sue felt almost impatient as she sat before the mirror and set her hair. This bedroom of hers was turning into a worrying room for sure. Dave hadn't mentioned any plans for the evening. Most of the time, she knew, he stayed home. But he still saw the gang. Did he think they were wonderful guys? Mo—and the others? Or was he as disillusioned as she was? Ever since she'd become involved with the Jay Dees, it seemed, she had something to worry about most of the time.

Sue climbed wearily into bed. Mom and Dad—they'd made this Jay Dee meeting the best ever. Maybe she, Sue Stevens, most insignificant of all members, could evoke a change in The Crowd's routine. Or would she have a chance at Maxine's party?

She tried to relax, to make herself fall asleep. But every time she dozed, she'd awaken with a start. Judy had done it again. Judy was giving her a dreadful night. Finally she gave up trying to sleep and took her pillow over to the window and leaned against the sill. She watched the stars fade and the first streaks of dawn light the sky. She heard the birds begin their morning chatter. This was going to be a beautiful day. She was silly to let Judy worry her. Now the sky was as pink as her dress. If only she could write a poem about it. *Pink and blue, grass wet with dew . . .* poetry was not her line, that was for sure. The thump of the morning paper hitting the front steps broke her reverie and she hurried down the stairs. She felt almost disloyal to Dave as she picked up the paper. Judy had just been talking. She was sure of that now. The cement was cold against her feet as she stood in the doorway and read the front-page stories. A train wreck . . . a new conference . . . She breathed a sigh of relief. Then a smaller item toward the corner of the page caught her eye. *"Vandals Work Havoc"*— Taft Junior High—her school—had been broken in to. Windows were smashed and dynamite caps had blown up the fixtures in the boys' lounge. Teen-agers, the police suspected. *Mo, maybe? Dave, too?* Would Dave go along with the gang to destroy like that? Would he—or *could* he "chicken out" on a gang "project"? If he did, he'd lose his leadership for sure. Did it mean that much to him? The early-morning sunshine made the dew on the lawn glisten, but the day ahead looked like a bleak, formidable one. There was a decision Sue had to make.

18

Accused

SUE FACED THE DAY with dread and foreboding. She must see Dave. Her mind was made up. But Dave didn't seem to be at school. Neither was Mo, for that matter. Could they be "in conference" with Mr. Mack? She didn't envy them. Even though they had it coming.

She looked for Dave in the emergency assembly. Surely he wouldn't *still* be in the office—not with Mr. Mack standing on the stage, ready to address the student body.

Mr. Mack's voice betrayed his controlled fury as he addressed the youngsters. "An inside job," he called it, recounting the specific damage done to the building. "A disgrace to the school, a blot to the community." The chief of police made a speech, too. He told the students the police would welcome any information—even though the police department had some valuable clues as to the identity of the culprits. The guilty party would be discovered in time, he explained, but both work and money could be saved if students would only tell what they know.

"For instance," he said, holding aloft an object, "this key ring was found in the boys' washroom. Does anyone know whose it is?"

As he held it up to the audience, Sue felt sick all over. The tiny harmonica attached to the ring was a dead giveaway. *Dave, how could you,* she wanted to cry.

The assembly was finally over. Students made their way in excited groups back to their home rooms. Judy pushed against Sue at the doorway.

"Know where Dave was last night?" she asked. Her smile was a gloating thing. Sue didn't answer but pushed forward with the crowd until there were several students between Judy and her.

Back to the home room at last, Sue took her seat gratefully. But Mr. Henderson apparently thought the students needed to hear more on the subject of vandalism. *Americanism, patriotism, the business of living with oneself.* She studied her hands as she clenched them together. Was he lecturing *just her?* How were the other students taking it? She stole a glance at the student across from her and met a speculative grin. Quickly she looked to the other side. She was being watched—probably by everyone in the room. Her face felt like a mask. "Stop looking at me," she wanted to scream. "I didn't do anything."

By lunch time Sue was so unnerved she asked Mr. Henderson if she could remain in class during the hour.

"Perhaps you should see the school nurse," Mr. Henderson suggested. "You might be better off at home."

There was nothing Sue would like more than to be home right that minute. But she shook her head. "I—I just feel tired," she said.

If she'd had any doubts that rumors were flying and her classmates were regarding her with speculative interest, by the time afternoon classes were underway they were thoroughly dispelled. If students were talking, what would Mr. Mack be thinking? Sue fully expected a summons to his office. She could hardly believe her good luck when the dismissal bell rang and she was on her way home, free and unquestioned.

If only Mom were still driving her to and from school! But no, since the beginning of the week she was navigating to and from school on her own. Sue hurried down the block. With a start, she saw Dave waiting for her on the corner. She averted her eyes. She'd been looking for Dave all day. Now that he was here before her, she wanted to avoid him.

"Hey, Sue!" Dave grabbed her arm and pulled her to a halt.

Sue faced him. So okay, she'd get it over with right now. She looked at him and her eyes widened in amazement. He looked so excited, delighted. He seemed so smugly pleased with himself.

"Boy, what excitement last night." Dave gave an exaggerated sigh. "I'm really bushed."

Sue's eyes narrowed. "I don't doubt it," she said, her voice dripping with as much sarcasm as she could muster.

"Huh?" Dave's face looked a little crestfallen. "You know about it?"

"Who doesn't? It's all over school."

"All over school?" Dave frowned.

"How could you be so stupid?" Sue's chin jutted out as she lashed at him. "How can you possibly be such a dope? The harmonica on the key ring is a giveaway."

"Key ring?" Dave's air of mystification seemed so sincere, Sue felt as though he should get an "A" in acting ability. "I was going to tell you—I lost it."

"Oh, Dave." Sue's voice showed her complete scorn. "That's such a weak excuse. You're dumber than I thought." She jerked his bracelet off her arm and thrust it at him. "Here," she said. "This time we're really through. I'm quitting Jay Dees, too. I'm not having anything to do with any of you. I'm finished." She thrust the bracelet at him again. "Aren't you going to take it?"

Dave took the bracelet slowly. He stared at her with complete disbelief.

She brushed angrily at the tears that had sprung to her

eyes. "And don't look so stupid, standing there with your mouth hanging open," she stormed. "Maybe Judy will be impressed. I'm not." She turned on her heel and broke into a run. If she'd stayed there one more minute she would have been crying. After just a few steps she remembered doctor's orders and slowed her pace. She turned back once. Dave was still standing there at the corner. "Hey, Dave," he heard Judy call. She turned back quickly. It was all over. Judy and Dave—they deserved each other—destructive vandals!

It was almost too much of a coincidence as she rounded the corner to see Ricky and Chester walking ahead of her. She hadn't really talked to them since the day in her room. Maybe they'd be friends again. "Wait," she called. "Ricky, Chester, wait."

They turned, hesitated for a moment, then walked slowly toward her.

"What's the idea?" Ricky asked.

"I thought maybe—well, Mom probably made cookies or something today, and—would you—would you like some?"

"At *your* house?" Chester looked worried.

"You used to," Sue said. She raised her arm. "No bracelet," she explained. She knew she was being "pushy"—positively brazen. But she needed company.

"Okay," Ricky reached for her books. "I'm game."

Now that they were walking with her, Sue couldn't think of a thing to say. The boys couldn't, either, apparently.

Chester broke the silence once. "Say, that was sure something the kids did to the school," he commented. "Hope they all get caught."

"Yes." Now what had she meant by that, Sue wondered to herself. "Yes" for it being something—or "yes" for the kids getting caught. Her eyes stung. Somehow she couldn't see Dave facing the police. She continued the rest of the walk home in silence.

"That you, Sue?" Mom called as Sue opened the front door.

"Uh-huh," Sue made her voice gay. "And I've brought company."

"I expected you to. I made gingerbread to celebrate." Mom emerged from the kitchen, a broad grin on her face. She looked startled when she saw Ricky and Chester. "Why—welcome," she said. "I haven't seen you boys for ages." She turned puzzled eyes toward Sue. "Did you see Dave?" she asked.

Sue nodded. "Yes," she said shortly.

"Oh." Mom continued to eye Sue with a puzzled expression as she went about the business of cutting and serving the gingerbread. "Well, aren't you excited?"

Now it was Sue's turn to be puzzled. What in the world

was Mom driving at? Ricky and Chester maintained a discreet silence as they ate their gingerbread.

"Well, aren't you?" Mom pursued.

The back door banged and Kit and Jay came charging into the kitchen. "Gingerbread for us, too, Mom," Jay demanded. He gave Ricky and Chester a surprised look. "You here?" he questioned. He turned to Sue. "Where's Dave?"

"Two babies," Kit exclaimed. "Two whole itsy-bitsy babies."

"Yeah." Jay spread his fingers and shrugged. "Too bad one had to be a girl, but—"

"I'm glad one's a girl," Kit interrupted. "Girls are best."

"You mean," Sue said slowly, "that—Mrs. Young . . ." Her voice faltered.

"Sue," Mom studied Sue's face. "Didn't Dave tell you that Mrs. Young had twins last night?"

Sue shook her head. She hadn't given Dave a chance to tell her anything.

"Say, that's pretty great," Ricky remarked. "Two kids to boss around."

Sue stared at her plate woodenly. The others kept up a steady chatter and didn't seem to notice her silence. Why did it take the boys so long to finish a piece of gingerbread and drink some milk? Why didn't they leave? At last Chester had meticulously consumed the last crumb and the boys stood up.

"Guess we'd better start for home," Ricky said. "Thanks for the gingerbread."

"Sure was good, Mrs. Stevens." Chester shifted his weight from one foot to the other, and Sue wanted to scream her impatience at them. Why didn't they leave right *now*?

At last they were walking down the sidewalk. Sue felt dull and stupid as she turned from the door. Mom looked at her expectantly.

"Would you like to talk things out, Sue," Mom asked. Her eyes were warm and understanding.

"There's nothing to talk out, Mom," Sue said dismally. "I just goofed."

"About Dave?"

Sue nodded.

"But Dave and his dad were so excited when they stopped by. Why, Dave was a regular clock watcher as he waited for the exact minute when his father could drive him to school to meet you."

Sue felt tears spring to her eyes. "I—I want to go to my room now," she said.

"Sue, darling—" Mom made a gesture as though she were going to envelope Sue in her arms.

"Please, Mom." Sue's voice cracked on a sob and she hurried up the stairs. Sympathy! She couldn't stand it. Not after the way she'd acted the fool. She flung herself across the bed and let the tears come. Poor Dave. Why hadn't she listened, just given him a chance? But the key chain—the harmonica—they'd thrown her off. Was that what they had been supposed to do? To put authorities on the wrong trail? Once more Dave had an alibi. But how long would his luck last?

Maybe she should tell Dave—explain about the assembly—explain that earlier warning from Mr. Mack. Dave was home now, most likely. She could phone. She'd change her clothes, wash her face, and then phone.

As she reached into the back of the closet for her favorite old jeans, she noticed a couple of her dresses had slipped from their hangers and were crumpled on the floor. She picked them up. The pink dress—how could it have fallen down? She shook it out. The lovely, swirly skirt was wrinkled, unfresh looking. Now it would have to be laundered before she could wear it. And then its pretty newness would never be the same. Slowly she dropped it in the hamper. Her pink dress, her lovely, lovely pink dress, the one Dave liked so much . . . Would he ever like it—or her—again?

Sue walked down the stairs and over to the phone. "I'm going to call Dave," she told her mother. "I have something to explain."

Her fingers were wooden sticks as she dialed. She heard the phone ring . . . one . . . two . . . three . . . on the ninth ring, she heard the receiver picked up.

"Hello?"

Sue swallowed. "Mr. Young," she said, her voice a mere whisper.

"Hello, hello," Mr. Young repeated. "Speak louder. I can't hear you."

"This is Sue," she said. "May I speak to Dave?"

"Just a moment."

Sue heard his footsteps recede across the floor. Her heart was hammering so loudly she hoped Dave wouldn't be able to hear it. The steps were coming back again. *This is it,* she thought desperately.

"Sue?"

"Dave," she started, then stopped short.

"This is Mr. Young, Sue." Dave's father's voice was kindly, almost pitying. "We were just leaving for dinner when you called. Dave said he'll try to phone you when we return home."

"Thank you." Sue hung up the receiver and stared at it numbly. Dave wouldn't call. He was telling her in no uncertain terms he was through. Her steps lagged as she walked to the kitchen. "Dave—Dave was outside," she told her mother. "Maybe—maybe I'd better explain."

19

Kangaroo Court

SUE SPENT A BAD night. Even telling Mom—and then Dad—about everything hadn't helped much.

Now as she sat in class, half listening to Mr. Henderson, she tried to recall Mom's parting words. Mom and Dad were great ones for adages or proverbs or whatever one called them. Such as: It's always darkest before dawn, and every cloud has a silver lining.

"Sue," Mom had said as Sue started for school. "I know you won't believe this, but things do work out. They are never as bad as they seem."

Oh, but they were. If anything, they were getting worse. The disruption and excitement of yesterday had simmered down, but Sue was positive her classmates were eying her with curiosity. Or were they pitying her because she no longer wore Dave's bracelet? Perhaps she could apologize to Dave today, because he hadn't called back last night.

"Sue Stevens."

Sue raised startled eyes to Mr. Henderson.

"I'm glad you are finally with us," he said sarcastically. "I've spoken to you twice already. Would you care to put the problem on the board?"

Sue flushed miserably. What problem?

"Page eighty," she heard the girl behind her whisper. "The third one."

Sue flashed a grateful look to the girl as she took her book and walked to the blackboard. But once there, she wished herself fervently back in her seat. The formula for this problem completely eluded her. "I don't get it," she finally admitted.

"Obviously." Mr. Henderson's voice showed his displeasure. "Perhaps if you spent more time on your studies, and less daydreaming . . ." His words hung there, his thought uncompleted as Sue took her seat.

By the time lunch hour arrived, Sue knew today was a very bad day. Probably one of the worst. Mr. Henderson's stopping her at the door hadn't helped matters.

"Your work is slipping badly," he said. "You're going to have to dig in."

"I'll—I'll do better," Sue promised. She hurried from his disapproving gaze to the brick wall. She opened her lunch bag. One lone girl, one brick wall, one tuna sandwich; how had she, Sue Stevens, managed to get herself so unliked? Wasn't anyone going to join her? Had even Maxine deserted her? *Dave!* He was probably back with the gang, glad to be rid of her.

As she searched the yard for him, Sue's eyes widened in surprise. Instead of being with Judy and Mo and the others, he was talking to Chester and Ricky. She saw Cathy and Ellen join them and felt more lonely than ever. If only she had the courage to walk over and join them! She saw Judy go over toward them, too, then turn away and walk rapidly toward Mo. She wore that speculative expression on her face that Sue had come to hate. *Now what?*

Sue munched her sandwich thoughtfully. At least talking things out with Mom and Dad had eased her conscience. "We waited a long time for you to come to us, Sue," Dad had said. "We didn't want to pry."

"Parents are to help, darling," Mom had added. Both agreed her suspicions were well founded but not enough to relate to authorities. Dad had worried about the brass knuckles.

"If Mo has them," he said, "someone could really get hurt."

"I wonder why Dave became angry with Judy in the first place," Mom had wondered.

Now Sue puzzled over it, because if Dave hadn't gotten angry with Judy, none of this whole business would have involved her.

Afternoon classes seemed as dull as the morning's. Oh, to get home where she was *liked*. The final bell had never sounded so good. Sue gathered up her books and stopped by the music room for her violin. The load was heavy, but she could manage. As she reached the sidewalk, Judy and Laura fell in step beside her.

"What's the rush?" asked Judy. "We're having a special meeting of the Jay Dees. Didn't you hear?"

"You must come." Laura took a firm grip on Sue's arm.

"I've quit Jay Dees." Sue tried to shake off Laura's hold. "I'm going home."

"Later." Judy gripped Sue's other arm.

Now, instead of the usual route to either Judy's or Laura's, Sue saw the girls were steering her toward the hilly section in back of the school. "Where are we going?" she questioned. "What are we going to do up here?"

"You'll find out—soon." Judy's laugh was an ugly thing.

Sue glanced quickly over her shoulder. Other groups were trudging up the hill behind her.

"All the Jay Dees will be there," Judy promised. "This is going to be real fun."

A wild, nameless fear clawed at Sue. Her hands were clammy wet. Her legs were leaden weights as she plodded up the hill.

As they reached the crest and started down the other side, Sue saw that groups of youngsters had already congregated in the meadow-like clearing.

"I won't run away," she told Judy. "Let go."

Judy nodded to Laura and they both let go. "It wouldn't do you any good to try," Judy said.

Now that they had almost reached the clearing, Sue saw that The Crowd—the boys, that is—were waiting. Almost impatiently, it seemed. *Waiting and hating* was what the expression on Mo's face said. Other boys had congregated, too. But the only girls were the Jay Dees. Sue gave a start of surprise when she saw Ricky and Chester—and Dave. They looked as though they were being "guarded"—as she was?

Mo grinned broadly at Judy. "All set?" he asked.

"All set."

Mo raised his hand and a silence fell on the group. "Okay," he said. "We'll hold trial. But remember, guys, mum's the word—or else."

Maxine stood near Sue's elbow. "Isn't this exciting?" she whispered.

Sue couldn't answer. Her mouth felt parched. Her gaze riveted on Dave as he was pushed forward to stand before Mo. He shook off the hands of the boys. If he was afraid, his face didn't show it.

"This guy," said Mo with a wave of his arm toward Dave and then the crowd, "is yellow. Or maybe he'd rather be called chicken."

Dave's eyes narrowed. He shrugged disdainfully.

"Yellow."

"Chicken."

Sue felt her fury replace her fear as the others made a chant of the names.

"First witness," demanded Mo.

Sue stared in disbelief as Chester was led forward. His face was white with fear. His hands, Sue saw, were tied behind him. He stared at his feet.

"Tell us, Chester," Mo drawled, "don't you have proof Dave is chicken?"

Chester swallowed hard but no sound came. Finally he shook his head.

"Come on now, boy, be honest. Don't you remember your Sunday suit?" Mo jerked Chester's hands upward, and Chester winced. "Going to talk now?"

Chester shot a pleading look at Dave, but Dave's gaze was averted, as if he were oblivious of the crowd around him. Chester swallowed again. "You fellows," he began in a voice so low Sue had to strain forward to hear him, "started roughing me up one night. In a vacant garage, and you darned near ruined my suit, and . . ." His voice trailed off.

"And Dave, here, what did he do?"

Chester remained silent.

"He was chicken, wasn't he?" Mo jerked harder on Chester's arms, and the boy gave an involuntary gasp of pain. Ricky started forward as if to help, but the boys beside him held him back.

"For crying out loud!" Dave's voice was clear and strong. "Leave him alone, will you? I'll tell you what happened—as if you don't know. I faked my turn at roughing him and I showed him where to sneak out for home. So what?"

"So I didn't get my licks." Mo flushed angrily. "You played boy scout before I had my turn."

"So what?" Dave's voice showed his scorn. "I don't pick on kids who don't have a chance."

"Chicken, chicken, chicken." Mo's eyes blazed. "You're not calling the plays."

"Maybe I am."

"Well, kid, the master's voice." Mo turned on Chester, his voice sugar-sweet. "And may you be the first to lick his boots." He jerked viciously on Chester's arms, and this time Chester fell to his knees.

"Quit it." Dave shoved Mo aside and helped Chester to his feet. With deft fingers he untied the knot that held his hands. "If there's any bootlicking," he said to Mo, "you're the one to do it."

Mo started menacingly toward Dave. "You're too chicken to fight," he said, "or you'd stick 'em up right now."

Sue felt her heart pound as the two boys circled each other.

"This is what Mo was working for," Maxine whispered. "He's going to give Dave a real working over."

"With his knuckles it'll be easy," Judy whispered back.

Sue's stomach turned over as the impact of Judy's words hit her. Knuckles! *Brass* knuckles! "Stop it, stop it," she heard herself scream. "Dave, don't fight." In a flash she dumped her books and violin on the ground and started to run. Judy made a grab for her arm, but she shook it free.

"Lookit, lookit, Dave's girl's chicken too," Mo shouted. "She can't stand a fight."

Let them think what they wanted. She had to be in time. She had to, had to. Her legs were heavy, leaden pipes as she pounded to the crest. A pain in her side made her hold it, press against the scar with her hand. She couldn't stop now. *Don't run.* Silly, silly doctor. She had to run.

She raced down the hill toward the school. This was a nightmare of reality. This was living the dream where you couldn't run because your legs wouldn't go. She tripped over a slight raise in the sidewalk and stumbled to her knees. For a bad moment her knee felt paralyzed. Then she was pushing herself to her feet.

Step, step, run, run! Her throat was dry. Her heart pounded against her ribs. She could scarcely breathe. The school building which had stayed so far away now loomed before her. She pounded up the ramp, down the corridor. She banged with one hand against Mr. Mack's door as she opened it with the other.

"Stop them, stop them," she pleaded. "Mr. Mack, you've got to stop them. Mo has knuckles. He's going to hurt Dave. Over the hill."

Even as she cried out, Sue felt the room turn round and round. Mr. Mack's face spun weirdly before her. Her legs had turned to jelly. There was a strange singing in her ears, but through it all she heard another sound, the thin scream of a siren. Police . . . ambulance . . . *Dave. She'd been too late.* The floor pitched toward her, and Sue felt herself fall into a soft, cottony darkness.

20

One Rotten Apple

SHE FLOUNDERED THROUGH WAVES of low voices, and then a pungent, acrid odor brought her sharply to reality. She sat up wildly—she was on some sort of couch—and saw the familiar faces of Mr. Mack and the school nurse.

Reality! Dave! Mo! The brass knuckles!

"You didn't stop them." Sue heard her voice raise hysterically. "You didn't stop them."

"It's all right, Sue, everything is all right." Mr. Mack's voice was placating and Sue hated it.

"I told you," she said. "I told you to stop them. And you didn't. You said if I needed help—and you didn't."

"It's all right," Mr. Mack repeated. "The fight never happened. The police were waiting."

"The—police—were—there?"

"This is the break they wanted."

Sue looked at Mr. Mack blankly. His words weren't making sense. If the police had been there, why hadn't she seen them? If the police had been there, why had she come running to Mr. Mack, making a fool of herself?

"We've called your mother," the nurse said. "She'll be right over." She handed Mr. Mack a small, capped bottle. "Here, in case she feels faint again."

Spirits of ammonia Sue decided as the nurse left the room. None of that.

"I'm glad you came, Sue." Mr. Mack smiled down on her as he arranged some cushions on the couch. "You had to take the step."

Take the step? That she had. Maybe Mr. Mack was glad. She was heartsick. By turning "informer" she'd made sure no one would ever like her—or even speak to her, most likely—again.

"You've a badly skinned knee, young lady," Mr. Mack continued. "Perhaps I should dress it."

Sue shook her head. "Let Mom do it," she said.

Sue watched as Mr. Mack busied himself around the office. Dave—Mo—the rest of the kids—— "My violin and books are up there," she said suddenly.

"Everything will be taken care of. Don't worry."

Don't worry? That was easy to say. Mr. Mack wouldn't know what it was like to be friendless.

A sharp rap on the door—and Mom was in the office.

"Mom." Sue felt tears spring to her eyes. "Mom, Mo had the knuckles."

"He did? My goodness." Mom seemed to brush Sue's words aside as if they weren't important. "See if you can hurry, dear. The car's right outside, and I left the motor running." She held out her hand to help Sue to her feet.

"Need any help, Mrs. Stevens?"

Mom smiled. "No thanks, Mr. Mack. We can manage. And thank you so much for phoning."

Once they were in the car, Mom drove smoothly away from the school. How could she be so cool, calm, and collected? Sue felt anger in place of her tears. Or was that what Mom was striving for, to keep Sue from crying?

"Do you think they'll get in trouble, Mom?"

"I think you're all going to get in trouble," Mom answered smoothly, "before you get out of it."

All? Mom hadn't asked who "they" were, even. So she knew!

Mom wouldn't even talk about it when they arrived home. "More like a four-year-old than fourteen," she remarked as she applied antiseptic and bandage to Sue's knee.

Even when Dad came home for dinner, Mom kept the conversation light and fanciful. But after the dishes were done and they were all settled in the living room, the doorbell rang and Mom answered it as if she knew who'd be there.

Sue gasped as she saw a police officer walk into the room. Jay and Kit were wide-eyed when he asked Sue and her parents to be present in the judge's chambers at ten the next morning.

"This is your picture?" he asked Sue, showing her the photo Maxine's dad had taken initiation night. "You are a Jay Dee?"

Sue could only nod.

"Is Sue going to jail?" asked Jay after the officer left.

Dad shook his head. "No, she'll just have a few questions to answer."

"But I didn't do anything bad," Sue protested.

"It takes only one rotten apple, Sue, to spoil the barrel. That's what my grandmother always said."

For her appearance before the judge, Sue dressed with meticulous care. She marveled at her parents. They were so calm, seemingly unconcerned. She was shaky all over. Sue had scanned the morning paper thoroughly to see what mention was made of the "fight," but the story was small, crowded into capsule size by more important events. More important? How could anything be more important than this unpredictable day ahead. Yesterday she had hated school. Now the security of a classroom seemed good.

The judge's chambers were quite crowded when Sue and her parents arrived. Apparently the Stevens trio were among the last. Dave sat with his dad. He nodded briefly as they entered. What must Alison be feeling as she stayed confined in the hospital while all this furor went on?

There was hushed silence when the judge walked in. He looked kindly and gentle enough, but what must he be thinking? Sue reached for her father's hand. Funny how terribly necessary parents were right now. Maybe all the kids were feeling like this. Judy, Mo, Laura, Maxine—Sue checked them off a mental list. The Jay Dees and the boys in The Crowd were all here—with their parents.

With quiet probing, the judge talked to one and then another. It was as if he were putting together a jigsaw puzzle, with bits of information connecting with other bits. The picture of destruction emerged sharp and unlovely. The minor pilfering of the local stores, the petty defacing of property—they seemed to be the background scenery to the serious offenses. On these two—the damage to the Driscoll home and the school—Judy and Mo starred. In fact, they seemed to be the only performers. It wasn't that they "shouldered" the guilt bravely, but that they *bragged* about their "achievements." They looked hostile, defiant, and proud of themselves. They related with scorn how the others had "chickened" on the Driscoll home. Mo seemed quite pleased with his clever "plant" of Dave's key ring in the school washroom. Dave—well, Dave had been as uninvolved as she was in *all* the activities, and Sue'd believed him a ringleader.

The judge exploded only once, and that was when Mo's mother had interrupted his story to say placatingly to the judge, "Boys will be boys, you know." His thunderous reply had made Sue shake in her well-polished shoes.

As the judge proclaimed the punishments, Sue saw the bravado and sureness seep from Mo and Judy, leaving them as shaken and subdued as the rest of them. All the girls and boys present were to report to the city hall for the next two Saturdays to do any menial tasks assigned them. There would be, the judge assured them, plenty of windows to wash, walls to scrub, and lawns to rake. As for Judy and Mo—they had a choice. Either they and their parents would make full restitution for the property damage and they themselves would be put on probation for three months, or—Sue shuddered at the alternative—Judy would be sent to Los Guilicos, Mo to Log Cabin. The probation, the judge explained, meant reporting to him every Saturday—and he would assign them suitable work.

"This is a fine community," the judge concluded. "We have, for the most part, upright, honest citizens, young and old. We want no rotten apples."

21

The Pink Dress

SUE WALKED DOWN the courthouse steps between her mother and dad, chastened and subdued. How humiliated they must be to have to come to court like this.

"A fine judge and fair punishment," Mom said as Dad opened the car door for her.

"Those poor parents." Dad answered. "We can still be proud of our daughter." He glanced at the clock on the city hall tower. "Lunch, and then Sue can go to school."

School? This afternoon? How could she face them?

As Dad pulled into the driveway, Mrs. Cannon ran to meet them, a cake box in hand. "I've brought you a surprise, Sue," she said. "You're such a brave, good girl."

Sue's mouth dropped open in astonishment. Good and brave? Was this more of Mrs. Cannon's sarcasm? But no, she seemed to mean it.

"I think you were wonderful to run for help," she said. "I always say you are a girl parents can be proud of."

Sue thanked Mrs. Cannon duly for the cake and followed her parents into the house. It was sort of symbolic, this cake. Which layer was she now?

She was cutting a second piece for Dad when the phone rang. "It's for you," Dad announced. "Dave, I think."

Sue talked briefly, then put the receiver back gently in its cradle. As she turned from the phone, she couldn't stop her face from smiling. "Dave's dad will pick me up," she said. "Dave has to go to school this afternoon, too." She looked shyly at Mom. "He—he wants me to wear my pink dress."

"It's all ready to iron, just take a few minutes," Mom promised.

The dress swished prettily as Sue walked beside Dave to the car.

"Quite a morning," Mr. Young commented. "You two were lucky."

Sue nodded. It was and they were!

"Thanks, Sue—for yesterday." As Dave spoke, his face turned a bright red. He held out his bracelet. "Wear this?"

Sue put out her arm and Dave fastened it around her wrist once more. "I'm sorry I doubted you—ever," she said simply. "I won't again."

When Mr. Young dropped them off at school, they were almost immediately surrounded by their fellow students. "Was it bad?" they demanded. "Tell us."

"It wasn't good," Dave said. "We don't want to talk about it." With his hand on Sue's shoulder, Dave wove deftly through the throng.

"Hey."

Sue saw Ricky and Chester run toward them. "Wait up."

Dave paused. "Nice guy, that Ricky. Chester's okay, too, I guess." He laughed. "You know, if it hadn't been for Chester, I might never have really known you. I got mad at Judy that night because she called me 'chicken' about him."

As Dave turned to greet the two boys, Sue saw Cathy and Ellen across the yard. They waved at her and she waved back. Why, they were coming over! Now they were smiling as though—as though nothing had ever happened.

"You were great, going for help," Cathy said. Ellen's round face beamed her approval too. Why—why they were liking her again.

"I don't know," Dave was saying. "I don't know if Sue's parents will let her go to the show with me."

"Sure they will." Sue smiled at them all. "But why not come over tonight and just listen to records—the six of us?"

"Sounds good," Ricky smiled. "If it's okay with your folks—and Cathy."

Cathy beamed, and Sue knew it would be okay with her. Just then Sue saw Mr. Mack approach them. "Could you two come to my office?" he said, "right now?"

Sue and Dave followed Mr. Mack down the corridor.

"Maybe I'm breaking precedent," Mr. Mack said as

soon as they were in his office, "but I'd like you two on traffic if you will."

Sue looked at Dave. There'd been a time, she was sure, when he would scorn this job. Now his face broke into a smile. "Sounds great, sir," he said.

"And you?" Mr. Mack turned to Sue.

"I—you know I want traffic."

"Start tomorrow at the south corner." Mr. Mack held out his hand and Dave and Sue shook it. "Taft can be proud of you two," he said.

As they left the office and walked down the corridor, Dave put his hand on her shoulder and stopped her. "That pink dress," he said. "Wear it always. It's good luck."

Sue laughed out loud. *Wear it always.* Just like a boy. They walked into the schoolyard together, and the whole world looked beautiful. More beautiful than ever before. Like the day after a storm when everything was washed clean . . .

About the Author

ANNE ALEXANDER wrote *The Pink Dress* when her youngest daughter was a middle school student, her middle daughter was in college, and her eldest daughter was the mother of two young children. It was the first of six novels inspired by personal experience and insight into the struggles and triumphs of her family. First published in 1959, *The Pink Dress* was an instant "must read" for girls. Over the years, the book has become a coming-of-age classic. Mrs. Alexander also authored several books for young children, including *ABC of Cars and Trucks* and *Noise in the Night*.

Anne Alexander was born in Shanghai, the daughter of an American missionary nurse and the British-Chinese captain of a Yangtze river boat. She grew up in the hills above Chung King, China, until her mother brought her to America when she was twelve. Mrs. Alexander was married for 66 years to her husband, Charles, a journalist with *The San Francisco Chronicle*. She was a beloved matriarch, an accomplished violinist, and a progressive thinker. Mrs. Alexander died in 2006 at age 92.